WHEN YOU
LIVE BY
A RIVER

WHEN YOU LIVE BY A RIVER

A Novel

Mermer Blakeslee

OPEN ROAD

INTEGRATED MEDIA
NEW YORK

Copyright © 2012 by Mermer Blakeslee

ISBN: 978-1-5040-9050-6

This edition published in 2024 by Open Road Integrated Media, Inc.
180 Maiden Lane
New York, NY 10038
www.openroadmedia.com

For the drowned farms of the Catskill Mountains

In memory of Osmer, Robert Norman, and
Josephine Nolan Blakeslee

WHEN YOU
LIVE BY
A RIVER

Out beyond ideas of wrongdoing and rightdoing, there is a field. I'll meet you there.

—Rumi (translated by John Moyne and Coleman Barks)

PART I

When you live by a river, you never ask what's the worst that can happen. You're always on watch—not on edge, but on watch, like standing around a cow or a workhorse, if you're what Mama calls a big-animal person. On account of their size, you stay alert, but easy too—not like small-animal people or what she calls city: lurching between too nervous and too carefree. The river, the East Branch, was just a tributary that most of the time meandered along at her own slow pace, here and there soaking a few fields and leaving behind a layer of silt. But any moment she could rise up and show herself to be mighty, what Reverend Sims called the doings of the Lord, but what I called, being only fifteen, All-That-Ain't-Me.

Digger, who I first knew as Uncle Willis, said I called it that because I was young, still thinking I was the center of things. He was forty-one years old and called it the World, but not the world you step over. He said the word hushed, like it was holy, his hand rising each time. He meant the World you've got to respond to, the World that comes and shapes your life and everyone else's. Even though Digger was a man of religion, quoting out of the Book, he didn't see eye to eye with Reverend Sims and wouldn't go to church. He said the reverend treated God like One Big

Holier-than-thou Shine who blinded out everything else. And Digger's God didn't shine. He stepped right in with the others: the river when it moved mighty, the World all hushed, and what Digger called death: God speaking.

Digger was a river person. His farm where he lived his whole life lay along her west bank for nearly half a mile. And even after he'd fall asleep sitting in his chair, he could hear the smallest sound. The dog would start up and I'd go to the window thinking maybe the water was rising, and he'd say, almost part of a snore, "Ain't nothing but some field mouse gettin' killed." And there I was acting city. But I had just moved there, three days after God spoke and Digger's wife, Aunt Addie, died.

We—my sisters and me—were called hill girls in school, everyone who lived up from the bottomland was hill. And we lived all the way at the top of Mary Smith Road in what was named Orson Hollow for the family who died there from the Spanish flu in 1918. A year later my parents moved in, and my mother, already with two young children and large with her third, scrubbed floors, walls, and ceilings with scalding water and alcohol and laid out on each windowsill a jar-top of sulfur to burn every night for a month.

They always said up there in the hollow, there were three stone for every dirt. But we always added on to the number when we worked, three stone for every dirt, then four stone, and soon, after an hour of hoeing, we were up to eighty-seven, eighty-eight stone—we never got much higher, though, we'd stop and take a drink where we kept water under a maple. There were maples everywhere, sprouting up even out of the stone walls lining the fields. And though that meant we always had a load of syrup, like everything maples made you pay. In a hard year, the corn shriveled up near the walls because the maples' shallow roots kept the dirt on either side dry as the stone.

Farm's so poor, Uncle Osmer would joke when the family got together for Christmas—everyone except Daddy who had gone off logging—farm's so poor, grasshoppers need a knapsack to cross it. My uncles would laugh every time, like Osmer made it up new right then. And even after they were only chuckling a bit, if anyone repeated, farm's so poor, that'd be enough to start them all up again, and most times, I couldn't help laughing too. But the joke was on me, farm's so poor was the main reason my mother gave me to Digger.

1

Everyone else was asleep when Leenie heard the trot, a grand trot, coming up their road, winter shoes hitting the stones. The neighbor's stud snorted outside the barn, and Leenie sat up, poked Frances next to her, and dragged her out of bed. They put on both their pairs of leggings and Leenie grabbed her Daddy's sweater from the clothes pole. He had gone off logging for the winter, leaving what he called his house of girls, Mama and their five daughters, and declaring Leenie, the oldest, "fortunate enough" to head up most of the work. Frances, two years younger, kept squinting through the dark at her sister as they dressed—she didn't know what Leenie was thinking and didn't dare whisper. Leenie mouthed, "Just come on." Everyone was still sleep-breathing—Janey and Mary in the other bed and Ma with little Emma across the hall. Leenie and Frances stepped down the stairs, skipping the noisy ones, crossed over Lazy, their dog, in the kitchen, and went out the back door. There was just enough moon not to bother with a lantern.

They saw the stud canter around the barn, a chestnut, his tail-bone straight up like a post. In one stride, he leaped onto the hay ramp and off again, over the grass where the scythe missed. The ground smelled cold, smelled frozen, but it was still soft enough

9

to give—he was leaving hoofprints in the dirt. He circled closer, facing in, crossing his hind legs so he could keep an eye on them. Leenie could feel the blood rush into her face. It really *was* Charlie Owen's prize—full of sweat, but not a cut on him.

"Frances! Halter up Lady. Put the chain over her nose."

"Leenie, you ain't thinkin'—"

"I certainly *am* thinkin'."

"Well, what about Ma? Why ain't she out here? She ain't even been *asked*."

"Frances," Leenie said, her voice turning real quiet, "Frances." She felt the name wrap around her sister. Ever since she could remember, she had used it as her lasso. "Frances," she repeated again and her sister turned, pulled back the door, and though the moonlight didn't reach into the barn, Frances knew where the lead chain hung.

He cantered by Leenie again, his back rounded, his gait easy. Then he stopped and turned toward her, snorting, reaching with his nostrils into the air, smelling her, smelling Lady. Leenie didn't dare look him in the eye. She stared instead at his shoulder, it had a good strong slope to it. He had a finer head and neck than Lady, high withers, a broad chest, though he was leaner through the body and with longer legs, some thoroughbred in his line. It was hard to tell how tall he was, he carried himself tall, 17 hands probably. Lady was shorter, only 15.2, half-Belgian, half-nothing, steady, stout, a heavy winter coat and good feet. Daddy had called her Lady-God-Bless, which started out when he bought her as Lady-God-Bless-an-Easy-Keeper. Leenie could hear her back out of the stall, her steps on the cement, then on the ground, calm even though she was in heat, so calm it made Leenie pause. How could the mare *not* know what was in store?

"Bring her over here. The ground's flatter."

As Frances turned Lady around, the stud jumped sideways

WHEN YOU LIVE BY A RIVER

and took off toward the hay ramp before he circled again. Still snorting, farting, he paced back and forth by the water trough, his poll arched and his head proud. "Talk to her, Frances. Keep the chain snug. And don't let her jump forward." Leenie patted her flank. The mare swung her hind quarters toward him. "There's a girl," Leenie said, "there's a girl," and laid her hand hard against Lady's rump so she wouldn't push into her. "Easy, easy girl." She lifted her tail. Still in heat. She could smell it against the cold, sour like silage or wet leaves. This was more than luck, this was *fate*—the first time she ever thought that word.

The stud was full of it now, cantering back and forth, his nostrils flared, his haunches well under him. He'd stop only to set his back end down, pitch his front feet side to side. Leenie saw the glint of his shoes in the moon. Winter shoes. He's going to scrape her back! He reared up, but he wasn't coming any closer. "Come on," she said under her breath, "come on in." But he kept circling.

Leenie could hear Frances. "Stop whimperin'," Leenie said. "You got the *chain*. You just gotta hold her." But just then he lunged toward them, and Leenie jumped away. He reared, straddled his legs over Lady's back. She sunk some but her hind legs held as she set herself against him. "Hold her steady," Leenie said, "talk to her." But Frances was still whimpering. The mare swung and he fell off her hind end.

"Leenie!" Frances screamed. "Watch it!"

"Shush. I'm lookin' out."

He didn't back off. He pushed on her tail with his nose, swerving side to side behind her, trotting in place, making squeals that sounded more like a hurt hog than a horse. Going to wake up Ma, Leenie thought. His chest and shoulder were soaked with sweat, even though his coat wasn't half as heavy as the mare's. He was springing up off his hindquarters, ready to mount Lady again and Leenie backed away as he reared up.

It was hard to tell then what was him or what was Lady, even though she was darker and had a black tail.

"Now hold her *there,* Frances, and stop your tremblin.'" He was humping her rump, his back rounded and thrashing, but he hadn't found her, he wasn't inside her. His hind feet kept lurching forward, trying to get in closer. Leenie could see drips of blood on Lady's side from where his shoes grazed. She'd have to be quick, like Charlie Owen had been that once, while she and her daddy leaned up against the fence. She came in close by his shoulder. All she could smell was sweat, wet hair, Lady's juice squirting, and then she saw it, like a pole stuck straight out from his belly. She ducked in and grabbed it. It was hot and hard too, but not like wood or stone or metal, it was like nothing she ever felt before. It was hard because it was alive inside, too alive for what was holding it, the stretched skin. Leenie reached with her other hand for Lady's tail, her black tail darker than the rest of the night. In a flash she saw the blood red of her hole and as Lady set her hind feet, she shoved it in. At first Lady seemed too small, but once it broke through, it was easy, it kept going in, it was easy because just like the half-frozen dirt, Lady held her ground just enough and just enough gave way.

"What's got into you?" Leenie whispered to Frances after they were safe and warm in bed, Lady back in her stall and the stud gone. It took only a few stones and he was down the road and across the creek. "What's got into you? You gotta calm yourself." But as Leenie said it, she knew the word calm had changed for her. It was colored now with the mare, how she had walked out of her stall into the night, she was so steady, with her stocky body and thick coat. Lifting her tail had been like opening the door to the stove, looking into that small red hole flaring. Leenie could still feel the heat. She wasn't afraid of it, though, and hadn't been then. "It's just animals," she whispered as she squeezed Frances, still shaking, against her. Her sister was bigger than Leenie had been at thirteen, with bigger muscles and breasts already, almost as full as hers. Daddy called Frances "the impetuous one," but it was only true during the day.

The next morning Leenie thought up the perfect excuse to scuff out all the hoofprints they found on the road. The two girls would go down to the front pasture to check the fence, the locust posts they had set in as deep as they could the week before. But it didn't turn out an excuse. As soon as they rounded the corner, they stood looking at a whole morning of extra work— two posts leaning almost horizontal, only three strands of wire holding them up, as if the rocks they had wedged them in with had been made of sand. Goddamn cows, Leenie thought, feeling like her daddy. Once they see that green, silky grass rising from the drainage ditch when everything on their side's brown, they start pushing, slow and steady, they got all day to push.

Leenie lifted up the nearest post and let it drop again, staring down at the long, skinny hole. *Where ground gives.* Words would often come to her like that. Like people, she imagined them, visiting, gathering in clusters after church or a town supper. But something always brought her out again. Usually Frances. Leenie looked over at her. She was biting her thumbnail through the hole in Daddy's glove, her mouth puckering into a grin. The daytime Frances was back.

"Come on, Leenie!" she howled. "Come on, come on, come on!" and she stomped her feet till Leenie sang out a streak of "goddamns":

"Goddamn Goddamn Goddamn Goddaaaaaamn! the softened ground.

"Goddamn Goddamn Goddamn Goddaaaaaamn! the wrong side brown."

That was how they worked together every day, Frances howling, Leenie staring, then cussing a funny tune. Otherwise it'd be nothing but lists—chores, tools, crowbar, shovel, wire-pull, hammer, more fence nails—they could slog on forever and like their mama, maintain.

They weren't finished setting in the first post when Old Man Richard, the deliveryman, drove up. He came every day from Lloyd's down in Pepacton to take their order, every morning except Saturday, the day it was. Something was wrong. Leenie crossed over the ditch toward his truck and he stopped long enough to ask if her mother was home. She nodded toward the house. Frances fell in behind and they followed the dust up the road to hear the news.

Soon as they saw their mama's mouth as she stepped onto the back stoop, they knew it was a death. Frances thought it was their father, but Leenie never did. The whole time she knew it was her mama's youngest sister, Addie, giving birth, though they hadn't seen her since September when they took her all their baby clothes. But even as Leenie was guessing it, it came as a shock. Aunt Addie was younger than their ma by nine years and so strong and stout—not fat, stout—big legs, big shoulders, big arms, big wide jaw. *My wife can outwork most men,* Uncle Willis always bragged.

They followed Mama into the kitchen. As soon as she turned and said, "Addie," Frances pulled her arms in tight to hold herself and just before she seemed about to burst, ran out the back door. Mama lowered herself into a chair by the table and Leenie sat down across from her. Janey, only six, slinked into Leenie's lap. Mary, ten, carried Emma in from the front room. Like dogs, Leenie thought, how the little ones flock toward crying. But Mama wasn't crying, just sitting. Leenie didn't cry either, she stared down at the enamel—green lines curly-cued in a sea of cream—while Janey's face grew hot against her chest. *The air full of tears*—words flocked too, toward the heat. It was hard to look up at her ma, her face drawn, white, the life sucked right out. Leenie closed her eyes. Addie's face always seemed so alive, always too red from the sun, even in winter. She would break into a laugh or a snort, dancing around her kitchen, though the music she danced to she had to keep in her head because she was tone deaf, couldn't even sing "Happy Birthday," or especially "Happy Birthday." It was her present to you, she'd always say, *not* to sing out loud.

Pole opposites, her mama called them, because she'd never dance. Ma was the serious one, and skinny. Not frail though, she sure wasn't that, every fiber she had was stretched taut. Now she kept swallowing, and not one of them, not even little Emma, broke the quiet, they just watched their ma swallow as she rubbed the edge of the table with her fingers.

A few hours later Mama cranked up Uncle Osmer's Model T and took Leenie with her to the Van Hutton farm to call Daddy's boss in the Adirondacks, and it wasn't till Leenie heard her say into the phone: *Addie died giving birth. Baby's alive,* first to the boss's wife, and then again to the boss, who said he'd be going out by the end of the week to where the men worked, that she felt her mother lighten. Just knowing Daddy would be on the other end of that news made her ma turn to Mrs. Van Hutton, smile, and say *yes* to the cake and coffee she had refused when they first walked in. And Leenie saw too why it took so much to move Mama's face—except with Addie, she'd laugh with Addie— but at home, she was carrying a load, like Frances pouting just now being left with the work or last week Mary's glasses getting crushed or the cows still pushing over the new posts she and Frances spent two days hammering in. How all those daily things turned into secrets when she couldn't talk them out, not at night to Daddy, and not over a phone because most of them were too small to be news, but they still added up and grew hard. Like stones, Leenie thought. She saw her mama carrying one hundred stone for every dirt.

They rode home in silence. There was just a hint of snow, enough flakes to call attention to the air before they landed, disappeared. They came this way, south toward Roscoe, only when they had to go to Dr. Lathrop or to Sorkin's to buy cloth the few times feed sacks wouldn't do, though the mill had started to dye them and sometimes even made them in prints. They passed the Two Brothers' place (no one called them by their names), the huge oak in front growing sideways along the ground after it got split in two by lightning, then Mabel Earle's farm and the cemetery and the sawmill by the road up to Becker's, and still neither of them spoke. But just as they passed Charlie Owen's and turned on to Mary Smith Road, her ma said, facing straight ahead, "You're gonna have to help me get through this, Leenie."

"Alright," Leenie answered, though the word felt false. I'm a lie here, she thought and then wished she hadn't.

That afternoon, when Mama went to see Addie—all the way down on the far side of Pepacton—she didn't take Leenie but left both her and Frances to take care of everything—feed, milk, scrape the gutters, heat up supper, and of course keep Emma fed and dry—one of them couldn't have done it all. And even though Addie was already dead, Mama was in a hurry because she wanted to be alone with her as she was for a while, before the Daunton boys came to lay her out. Ma never stated how long she'd be, but they figured she'd sit watch most the night.

Just as Leenie was dishing up the potatoes and cabbage, Mary blurted out, "When's Lady gonna foal?" Frances, right across from her, gave her a look so mean Mary put down her milk, set her hands in her lap, and turned to Leenie, about to cry.

"It's fine, Mary, honey," Leenie said, "don't . . ."

Mary's shoulders dropped as she let out a long breath, though she was still holding in tears.

"A dream?" Leenie asked, but she knew even before her little sister nodded.

"But when I saw," Mary spoke so softly Leenie had to lower her ear, "when I saw Lady's sides, I knew it wasn't just a dream."

Mary had a lot of not-just-dreams she usually told only Leenie after she got called a tattle in school. She didn't try to be. She just didn't know what to keep in because she never knew what she really did know.

"Don't you say a word to Mama," Frances said and Mary nodded. "Not yet, she can't know yet. And that goes for you too, Janey." Janey's head was so close to her plate, you couldn't see the potatoes for her face. "Lift your head," Frances said, "you hear me? Don't say nothin'. It's a secret. *Leenie's* secret. Though once Ma sees what those shoes done . . ." Frances glared at Leenie.

"What'd you see in the dream, Mary?" Leenie asked.

"I seen . . ."

"I saw." She was always correcting her.

"I saw the chain. Frances holdin' Lady's head and I couldn't see where *you* were but I seen a lot of movin'. Saw it happened like dogs." She pushed her new glasses up to the top of her nose.

"They're just animals," Leenie said, and the echo of her own words comforted her.

After they ate supper, Leenie washed up while Frances went out to the cow barn for the final feed and to rub more bag balm on Lady's wounds. She didn't come in again till Leenie had already started to read the little ones to sleep. She crept in behind Janey, who was behind Mary, the three of them spooning in the bed as Leenie read Christina Rossetti, always a favorite, until they all fell asleep. Everyone except Emma, just a year and a half old, squirming this late without her ma. Leenie took her downstairs to rock her in front of the stove, staying clear of the noisy steps. Frances snuck down a little later, what their daddy called sleep-dreaming. She pulled a chair out from the wall and set it inside the light the lantern gave off from the top of the wood box. "You awake or asleep?" Leenie asked and Frances nodded. They sat there waiting, listening to the rough hum of the fire. Emma finally fell asleep. Frances's head fell forward and back till the crick in her neck woke her up again, enough to walk upstairs.

Leenie heard the car before Lazy did. Her mama opened the back door into the kitchen, shushing the dog even though he was only wagging. Leenie didn't get up, she didn't want to wake Emma, she'd been so fussy. The brush of her ma's footsteps in the dark made the night seem soft, like it couldn't do any harm. The fire was warm and Leenie sat there, excited all over, knowing she was about to be a surprise. And she was. "Leenie!" her ma whispered and stepped back when she saw her under the light. She sat down in the chair Frances left. Leenie didn't feel like her child then, just fifteen, she felt like an adult because she'd never sat in front of the stove with her ma alone before. She handed her over Emma, already damp again.

"Leenie," Mama started, as the baby settled into her, but then she stopped. Leenie opened the stove to load it up for the night, it could fit at least two more sticks of wood.

"Leenie," Mama said again. "Uncle Willis and I been talkin'. On account of your . . ." and she patted her head on the side, by the temple. "Willis made a promise. He's gonna send you to . . ." and she gathered herself, "college. Not now, of course. But when time's right. He's promised."

Leenie knew the words were supposed to make her happy. Maybe it was her mama's tone—not quite right, not *simple*. She felt the adult in her turn hard, preparing itself. The world outside—cold, dark—seemed too close. Her ma didn't say anything more. The creosote in the stovepipe popped, and the fire hummed.

Mama always said Leenie wasn't cut out to be a farm girl—she even called her a city girl like she was someone strange, a foreigner. City: lurching between too nervous and too carefree. But after a few years, Leenie stopped minding. Then she almost liked it—it was true and her ma just saw it first. Leenie had skipped three rows in the Mary Smith School—which meant three grades, each row was a grade—and left when she was only eleven to go to the high school down on Berry Brook. A bad fit right from the beginning, the kids being so much older. She graduated in June and hadn't missed it one iota. She read any time she wasn't working or braiding her sisters' hair or picking flowers and seed heads with Mary for the house. Leenie would sit down in her mama's chair (that her mama never used) and read. She liked poems best—Emily Dickinson, Walt Whitman, or the book Aunt Addie gave her: *Renascence* by Edna St. Vincent Millay. Sometimes, though, she wouldn't be reading, only repeating the words—just to hear them. Like with Shakespeare when Mr. Milford, her English teacher, gave her his copy of the *Sonnets* to take home. She'd recite over and over: "When yellow leaves, or none, or few, do hang / Upon those boughs which shake against the cold, / Bare ruin'd choirs, where late the sweet birds sang." Or she just touched the words with her fingertips—they felt real to her, like the words that came to her on their own—they were living, like seeds were living. But she didn't tell anyone these things. Mama and Frances would've rolled their eyes, adding that to her list of "quirks." She told Mary, though. Daddy had called Mary "the susceptible one" and now when Leenie said the word, she could see Mary's face, open like a field.

There was only one book Leenie wouldn't pick up. The Bible. Ma said it was because of Daddy, but Leenie wasn't so sure. You didn't have to be more than ten to know people quoted out of that book only when they were trying to prove you or someone else wrong, as if they themselves were the appointed messengers of God. They would sit there after their quote like they were bathing in its glow. She wouldn't ever claim the truth like that.

That was one thing about Uncle Willis, Addie's husband. Though he wouldn't step—not one toe—into church, he loved his Bible. That's why he talked like he was preaching and spoke out things about the world and about God she had never thought of. He didn't quote from the New Testament, he stuck to the Old. It never seemed to bother Addie much. She'd tease him, "Now, don't go carrying on again, Willis." Or she'd wink at one of them and say, "I just keep his mouth full if I want peace."

One time they pulled into his driveway and he was in the front yard looking up at the sky. Like he was a tourist, a summer boarder with no work to do. They hadn't seen him in maybe three months and he didn't say hello or even yell for Addie while they were piling out. He looked at them like they'd been there all along and said, "Most unnatural color, that sky, ain't it? Why in heaven would the Lord Above pick that blue?" He never cared about the science of it, he cared only that it *was*. "It's our job," he'd say, "to know how to look at what is, at the World, know how we're gonna associate with it." That floored Leenie. She never thought the sky or the ground or a tree trunk, whatever they were looking at, was something they had to figure out how to *associate* with. Sometimes, after Uncle Willis would bring what he called "a musing" to a close, Addie would look at him, pull back her head, and go, "Humph!" Then she'd look at Mama and the girls too, and say again, "Humph!"

* * *

Mama said the next morning, the morning after her news, while Leenie was mixing up food for the barn cats, low enough so only she could hear, that if she didn't go off to that "hu-minities school" and become a teacher, she'd amount to nothing, or maybe even worse, and though Mama didn't say what was worse than nothing for a girl with no means, Leenie knew.

"It's called college," Leenie said and turned away.

That afternoon, Mama went up to the attic and brought down the steamer trunk that came from Uncle Osmer after he worked the boats. And then just before supper, with some fanfare she wasn't usually prone to, she brought all the girls into her room and declared the trunk "belonged to Leenie."

Whatever could I fill that with? Leenie thought. Her clothes, books, even paper to write home with wouldn't fill a quarter of it. It wasn't till a little while later she wondered, Why now? I ain't going *yet*.

Frances noticed her mother's fanfare too. "It's 'cause no one in our family ever gone to college before," Frances said when they were haying in Lady for the night. They'd never even met anyone they liked who'd gone to college, not Miss Daniels or Mr. Totten, not the Smith boy. Well, Leenie sort of liked Mr. Milford and Frances sort of liked Dr. Lathrop and she really liked his son, George, but he left college after just a year and came home. "So he don't really count."

"How do you know I won't up and leave too, come home?"

Frances stopped, looked square at her, holding the hay off to the side. "You ain't gonna want to come home, Leenie, you know it, otherwise Mama wouldn't be actin' so, so, so . . . dramatic."

"She ain't actin' dramatic. She's just feelin' more 'cause of Aunt Addie dyin'."

"It ain't Addie, it's the thought of you goin' off. People say when the firstborn leaves, it's hardest on 'em."

"Is that so?" Leenie smirked. Frances was always quoting what people said, though mostly the people turned out to be just herself. Saying "people" lent her authority, which she needed now because she didn't know what Mama was feeling any more than Leenie did. All they knew was how she had sat down in front of that trunk, her fingers moving like they always did, tracing back and forth over the hinge. And how she handed Leenie the lock, then reached into her apron pocket and pulled out the key.

It wasn't till that night that Mama came into their room, after the little ones had gone to sleep, and Leenie and Frances were what they called "under the covers but not in bed," meaning they still had their clothes on, hadn't gone to the outhouse their one last time, it had turned so cold out. Soon as Ma came to the door Leenie said to herself, Something's wrong. Mama sent Frances to load the stove and bring in not only the night's wood but enough for the morning too. Frances stomped out of the room in a huff. Mama waited till she heard every stair stepped on before she sat down on Leenie's side of the bed, and said, "There's more'n what I told you." She stopped then till she saw Leenie was ready. "You're gonna first take care of Addie's baby girl."

She waited for Leenie to say something, but she didn't. Then Mama started in with the advice. "Now, don't you ever let water drop onto hot grease." Like Leenie was Mary's age. And she shouldn't prune Addie's roses a day before the first day of spring and how because she loved the smell of lilac indoors, she could take the little hammer they used to smash the stems. Leenie still didn't say anything. "And when the monthly blood comes, you got to throw an extra coat of lime over it religious or it'll draw coon." Then she stopped, stared at Leenie like she was going to ask her a question. But instead, she handed her what looked like a rag made of rough terry cloth that's been wrung out and dried in the sun. "You're gonna have to dry nurse. Only way you'll be able to quiet the baby. Even after they're fed, they need to suck." Then her voice went real low. "Start tonight rubbin' your nipples." And she showed how, her fist rubbing her dress pulled tight over her bosom. "Rub till you can't take it no more. But stop then. Don't make 'em bleed. Make sure they ain't ever bleedin'. Won't have time to heal once you start nursin'. Just let her suck like you really did have milk."

That's when it sunk in: Leenie saw a whole life stood between her and the word *college*. She was paying her way by taking care of Willis and Addie's baby, her new cousin, not even named before Addie died.

Mama saw it come to her.

"When?" Leenie asked.

"Day after tomorrow. Soon as they take Addie away to bury, Hettie's gonna bring the baby back."

Leenie didn't want to start the rubbing that night like she was supposed to, she didn't know how to do it without Frances seeing. Being two years younger, her sister was always curious, and if she saw how it smarted, she would've ripped that cloth right out of Leenie's hand and thrown it in the stove. Instead she crawled in next to Frances like they did every night of their lives but now Frances was curled away, knowing she'd been left out. Leenie laid her hand on Frances's back and stroked her hair, straight and so fine it still seemed like a child's.

"Day after tomorrow," Leenie whispered. And Frances buried her face in the pillow, her fists pressed against her head. Leenie put her cheek on her sister's fists, kissed them, trying to turn them into hands and fingers again.

"I'll write every day." She almost believed it. Frances's skin got wetter and wetter, her hair too.

"You gonna answer me?" she asked, and then again, "You gonna answer my letters?" Leenie asked until Frances's fists opened and Frances turned toward Leenie and sniffled and said, finally, "Yup."

"Every day?" Leenie just wanted one more yup.

Then Leenie promised she'd come home for good, she would, by next fall, by summer, by spring, maybe even by Christmas. Frances knew she was lying, but Leenie handed her the lie like she was handing her a gift and Frances took it, there was nothing else to take. And the thought came back to Leenie, it was all around her: *I'm a lie here.*

After Frances fell asleep, Leenie crept out of bed, opened the drawer where she'd put the cloth, lifted under her nightgown and scratched till she couldn't bear it anymore, first her left nipple and then her right and then the left again but not as long, she was scared it would start to bleed, she went back and forth, one to the other, it felt better than stopping, making the pain on both sides match the pain inside.

Two mornings later, when Leenie was walking up from the barn, she heard Mama scream at Mary, "Take your glasses off!" Leenie stopped, tilted her ear toward the kitchen, and heard Mary's whimper. Leenie closed her eyes. *Don't duck.* Ducking made her ma so mad she hit twice then and twice as hard. Mary's face was going to be all blotched now (some from the sting, but mostly from her tears), and for some reason when Mary cried, Ma's blood would boil even worse. Leenie dunked the bottom of her skirt into the rain barrel and hid behind the woodpile on the porch ready for her sister to burst out.

"Here, over here," Leenie whispered, and Mary, looking behind her, handed Leenie her glasses and dropped her face into the cold wet cloth.

WHEN YOU LIVE BY A RIVER

"It's alright, it's alright," Leenie whispered, rubbing her shoulders as Mary started to sob, her back heaving. They all took their turns, didn't they, whoever happened to be close by, helping their ma in what they called the war zone.

As soon as she could, Mary started explaining, "I couldn't keep up, the food mill's broken and I couldn't . . ."

"Shh shh," Leenie was keeping watch so they didn't get caught. "Shh, Mary, honey, it's alright now." Then she added, "It's the fourth." The fourth of November, their parents' anniversary, and their daddy hadn't been home for it in years.

"Well, what was yesterday, then? And the day before?" Both of Mary's fists kept opening and closing.

"I know, I know, but today she's in a rush to see Addie one more time before they take her and I'm leavin' and that's makin' her worse too."

Leenie spotted Janey shivering behind the lilac, glanced into the window, then waved her over. Janey ran up, gave Mary a hug, and fled. Gangin' up, as their ma would say.

Mary stopped crying and some of the blotching on her face started to fade, except on her left cheek—Leenie dabbed it with her skirt. "Still sting?"

Mary nodded. "What am I gonna do after you're gone?"

"You can still whisper all your secrets to me."

"But you won't be able to hear 'em down in the valley." Then she looked up. "Will you?"

Leenie smiled. "If I find a quiet enough place, I can."

Just then Mama yelled, "Mary!" And Mary ran in. Leenie swallowed. The red around her sister's eyes was going to give her away.

Leenie wanted her daddy there too, though who was she kidding, if he was home he'd be asleep or on his way to a drunk. But as it was now, he wouldn't know till spring that she had gone to Uncle Willis's. Just normal doin's, Ma would say about everything they thought he should know about. "And what would he do anyway? Can't come home till the ground thaws," which was only half true, but no one dared say a word or even give each other a look.

They lifted the trunk onto the backseat where her sisters usually sat and that started the girls up, kissing and hugging and squeezing hands and then kissing again. Finally Ma said, "Enough," and cranked the engine, her mouth hardening into a thin line. Sometimes she called the car Osmer's Revenge, Daddy being the brother Osmer most loved to hate. As soon as Lazy stopped running alongside and they couldn't see Janey and Mary (the blotches almost gone) waving behind them and Frances holding up Emma on her hip, tears started down Mama's cheeks, though not a muscle moved, not even her lips. And she never wiped them away so they dropped off her chin and hit her dress.

Leenie stared out the side at the woods, and the farms in between—Dot's uncle's, then Les Fenton's, his brother's, and then Al Bouw the Dutchman's. Most of the upper fields were frozen. They could run on them now, chunks of dirt kicking from their shoes like stones. But there were still a few of what they called lucky spots where the sun shone the longest each day. They knew every one of them on top of Mary Smith Hill. Janey would always run ahead, then stop and yell back when she reached one, stamping her feet trying to feel over and over the last softness of the ground before it sealed itself up.

Leenie didn't cry till she saw the river, saw it spread out brown and slow, like a big old leg thrown over the valley.

"I ain't a river person," she said, but her ma had stopped crying by then.

2

An altar of earth thou shalt make unto me, Willis repeated again and again, and a grave thou shall dig for thy dead. He gripped the pickax and swung, hit the dirt. This wasn't dirt. The bottomland had dirt, had soil even, but this, up in this hollow, was just rock, broken, shattered rock, a bit of leaf mold. Even with the frost, he could smell the dank rot of leaves. Every second or third hit, he felt the twinge through the wood into his wrist. Another rock. He sunk the pick in behind and under it, jerried the handle back and forth, pried it free from the matted roots, tossed it onto the pile. Two, maybe three strikes before he hit another. A steady crop. They too, blindly seeking Thy light. O Lord, have mercy.

He straightened, pushed back his cap, wiped his forehead. He was no longer young, was he, at forty-one, sweating even in the cold—not down to freezing, but near enough and the sun already halfway to the valley. He should've started earlier. Tomorrow was the wake and he wanted to bury her as soon as it was over. Before Edith and her oldest came. He wedged one foot against the side of the hole, the other planted on a rock at the bottom, a rock he wasn't ready for. Get the hole wider first, give himself some room, then go deeper, down to where the dirt was damper, colder. *Where Addie's cheek . . .* but God hath spoken, he could not follow her, he was the one left, cursed to dig this—please Lord—unforsaken hole. Do not forsake her now. He swung and the words *altar of earth* swung too, and they calmed him.

Like haying calmed him. The grasses—timothy, clover, alfalfa—falling into rows as he circled each field, each with its own roll and pitch and different hill to face. Or stretch of river.

For years, when he hayed the Shaver field he'd watch the town boys gather under the bridge. He'd come over the knoll on the west end and see some boy—gangly, shirtless—swing from the rope and let fly. Sometimes a few older girls squealed on the rocks below, water up to their ankles, their knees. Maybe one or two, either braver or hotter, waded in deeper, their skirts floating on the surface like lily pads.

But that one morning (was it already ten years ago?) the river was quiet. Only the whir of the cutter bar, the steady clink of the harness. All the sheep lined up in their church, their children squeezed into their Sunday shoes while he was doing the unthinkable—working. But the sun had come out after a rainy week and God with His infinitely practical mind knew it was a good day to hay. And to see her as well, a girl, maybe fifteen, sixteen, in a light-blue dress and bare feet. She carried the rope up the bank and turned on the ledge to face the river, and then— he was waiting—her straight white legs cut the air, her dress lifted behind her. He raised the cutter bar and steered the horses to the edge of the field. She stepped through the river mud and onto the rocks, her dress raining a circle of water around her feet. It was Judd Hansen's girl—breathing hard, her hair flat and dripping. He watched her breathing a long time. Five years before he saw her again, Miss Adelaide Hansen, no longer a girl.

The ring of her name made him grip the pick harder, too hard, like his father had for years till he was no longer able to open his hands enough to hold a cup. But *her* hand had opened. At the end, when he could still smell her hair soaked with sweat and pulled back off her face, his eyes following the line of her part like it was a crooked road he walked up and down. And then, startling him, her hand lifted from the sheet and landed, open, on his forearm . . . Where were the verses? He could repeat the verses. *For the Lord sayeth* . . .

He struck another rock, it barely shook. He hit down on either side to feel how far it spread, he'd need the crowbar for this one. And to think they called this a farm once. Abandoned, the upper farm came along with the bottomland his grandfather bought when he returned from the Civil War, and though the ridge sheltered them from the northeast, he had always considered the extra acreage a waste.

But no longer. After rising from Addie's body, he'd stood at the back door looking at the ridgeline against the early-morning sky, and it came to him that the upper hollow was the closest he had to wild. It was there he'd bury her. He left the milking to Burdett, his hired man, and stuck some jerky in his pocket. Though he couldn't face the thought of eating, he might be able to chew. It'd been a couple years since he'd climbed past the old sugar shack overgrown with thorn apple, its roof collapsed over the rusted pans. He could've used a scythe in the upper pastures, the hardhack and brambles closed in so thick. Nothing was left around the old foundation except apple trees, shorter, craggier every year, their brown, half-frozen apples squishing underfoot. How many years since they had stopped picking these? Even the early greens that came in August were more worm than fruit.

By late afternoon, tracking northwest, he'd given up finding a good site. But then the ground leveled a bit and he saw it, the stone, a slab jutting upright from the earth eight, ten feet, a shadberry sheltering it from behind. It stopped him, took his breath. And then, as if on their own, the verses came: *An altar of earth thou shalt make unto me . . .* Exodus 20, what he'd memorized as a boy. *Thou shalt not build it of hewn stone. For if thou lift thy tool upon it, thou hast desecrated it.* Thy tool. He understood. The church had been laid with hewn stone. Had been desecrated. But this stone shall not be cut, will remain naked, as she will be.

Yes, God hath spoken.

And it was fitting that the shadberry shielded it. Addie had always liked seeing them blossom, first thing in spring when everything else was gray (the only time you could spot the shad)—like large white hankies fallen willy-nilly onto the hillsides.

But now, knee-deep in the grave, he could see nothing but skeletons of trees, black trunks shooting upright with barely a leaf hanging, except on the beeches and oaks. He never noticed the brown of the oaks when he was young, favoring the reds and oranges flaming up from the maples, but finally, as a grown man, he'd come to love it.

He was thirty-six years old when he saw her again at a baseball game in the back of Harry Larkin's place. It was the first game of the summer, the creamery against the quarry boys—whoever won he didn't remember—he was about to leave after each inning but he kept seeing that same girl (Judd Hansen's girl) jump up from the grass, shouting and clenching her fists and chewing on her knuckles, and he wondered who it could be she cared so deeply about. (He shook his head when he learned later it wasn't anyone. She just loved baseball and as soon as she picked a team, due to nothing more than a color of a shirt or a smile, she'd be as loyal as if her father or brother or son, none of whom she had, were playing.) She wasn't beautiful, exactly, it was something else that drew his attention, a buoyancy, as if her body was packed cell for cell with more life than anyone else's.

His problem was he didn't know how to court a woman. He barely went anywhere aside from the creamery or Uriah's store and he couldn't dance and he didn't care much for the silent movies Clifford Dent had started showing in Fletcher Hall. But when Mary Sprague told him it was Miss Adelaide Hansen, and she worked at Scudder's boardinghouse, he drove there and nervously asked her if she wanted to walk or maybe just eat with him and with her one arm up against the door frame and her other hand on her hip, she laughed and said, "You don't have very much imagination, do you?"

But she said yes anyway, and he walked her around his farm, first along the riverbank under the elms and sycamores lining the water and then up to the pastures. Addie wanted to walk all the way up to the ridge, and from there they saw the railroad station and the little road behind the creamery and the south end of Main Street. The dogs in town took turns barking and Willis named each one and the family it belonged to. There was an ease to their talk, and an ease, as well, to their silences.

Her grave slowly spread around him, the pile of unearthed rock rising above him.

And the Lord sayeth, In whatever place I choose . . . Yes, God, the Chooser chooses and he, the digger, digs. Willis stopped and flung the pick above him. It had come, what he was afraid of, the unholy heat. He pulled himself out of the hole and yelled to the sky, "Is this your Great Plan, Lord?" He grabbed the shovel, took aim at a trunk—basswood, good-for-nothing tree—and hit it again and again, his hands, his forearms, and his shoulders throbbing, till the wood of the handle split, and he slid onto the ground.

She was gone. He let the cold of the earth seep into the backs of his legs. *If thou riseth up, thou shalt fall beneath His Wrath.*

How he hated Him, his God. Willis spat. Lord, if I could fight you . . . but he couldn't raise his fist or lift his eyes, for what was he now, a hunk of matter? He couldn't call himself Willis John, no, he was just *Digger* again, what his mother had called him as a boy when he began digging in the yard a hole that by the time he was twelve could have hidden a wagon. The name still suited him, didn't it, it gave him a job at least, a necessary job.

Lee Daunton's sons stopped by to hang the black crepe over the door and the porch piece too, boughs of yew and juniper berries. Freddie, the oldest, seventeen and in line for his father's business, did a final check on Addie in the parlor. He thought the casket should be lower and adjusted the gurney. "So when the women kneel," he explained to Digger.

In the same sober tone, Freddie's brother, Sherm, said, "People will start coming about one."

Digger nodded. He was leaning on this boy, Lee's youngest son, not more than ten, and maybe Sherm sensed it too. He didn't run out to the car like any other kid his age would but slowly walked down the driveway and after he climbed into Daunton's car, turned his head toward Digger and waved.

It was only midmorning and there was nothing left to do. Addie's grave was dug, the horses fed and let out, the cows fed and milked and let out, the chickens fed, the barn clean. Burdett, Digger's hired man, had stayed on an extra hour before he left for his job at the creamery. Digger couldn't face the kitchen just yet—Addie at the sink, her back to him, talking. So devious, his memory. He sat down on the back step, shielded his eyes from the sun. He could split some wood, he thought, as Teddy, his dog, came up to lick his face. The cookstove took only small sticks and they'd be feeding it all day.

He was still there in the shed attached to the back of the house, piles of stove wood all around, when Hettie Brower arrived with the baby and a big bag. She was seventy-two now and someone always gave her a ride, they'd pull over as soon as they spotted the green woolen coat she'd worn as long as anyone could remember, even in summer. She came into the wood-shed—only salesmen or travelers looking for a room walked to the front—set the bag down and stood for a moment adjusting to the darkness.

Digger swung his ax into the chopping block. "Just tell me what to do," he muttered and followed her up the step into the kitchen.

"First, you're gonna give your daughter a bath," and she handed him the bundle she was carrying that didn't look fat enough to hold a baby. "Careful of her head."

He pulled the blanket down behind her cap and set the baby in the crook of his arm. There she was, his daughter, three days old, smaller than a bag of beans. She was looking at him, but she was not looking *back* at him, stopping him with her eyes. No, her eyes were completely open, he could fall into them. His hands felt weak, as if they had lost all their blood.

"You'll catch on. You ain't the first man in this town to have to raise a girl. The two I knowed were better mothers than most women. Big men too." She checked the fire in the cookstove, it had burned down low enough. She set the pan of water on top. Two or three times she dipped her pinky in the water and shook her head. Then finally, she nodded.

He laid the baby on the table and unwrapped the blanket, unbuttoned her white linen nightgown—twice, maybe three times as long as she was—unpinned her diapers. He couldn't get used to her size, her little arms, little chest, toenails he had to squint to see. And her skin. He should rub bag balm on his calluses, they had gotten so hard, they might hurt her. He lowered her into the water, her tiny legs moving slowly, haphazardly—as if this world were nothing but water surrounding her, water warmed by a low fire, a hand holding her. "You're my Johnny-jump-up," he whispered, "my little Johnny-jump-up." She didn't start to fuss until he brought her out of the water and they dressed her, her mouth squishing into a radish while one of the bottles of milk Hettie brought from a few mothers in town warmed on the stove.

Once the baby was asleep, Digger sat in the parlor, across the room from where Addie was laid. He took a small whetstone from his pocket and spit on it, started sharpening his knife. It was Hettie's suggestion: Whittle until the men arrived. "Something to do." Hettie always seemed to know what to do. But most important, she was there. As she always was, at the births where she was wanted, at the deaths where no one else was wanted. Births or deaths, seemed like that was all there was now. The rest of life shrunken into a few, fleeting hours.

The women began arriving first, the ones who lived close enough to walk. Just as Hettie had said they would. Digger could hear each one whisper as they walked into the kitchen, "How is *he* doing?" They set the hot dishes onto the Hoosier in the corner—Elizabeth's scalloped potatoes, Cynthia's pea soup, Mary's beans, everything but Addie's oatmeal cake. He understood now why they say, *A house full of food but no smell of cooking.*

Their voices suddenly quieted when they saw the baby sleeping in the basket by the stove. He laid the stone down, felt the blade with his thumb, it was sharp enough now. The apple wood he had picked up from the orchard had a good bend to it where he could fashion a grip, one that felt right to hold and lean on. He started shaving. Maybe Hettie could use this walking stick, especially for the back roads.

How Hettie had tried. After the bleeding wouldn't stop and Hettie's helper lifted the baby from Addie's belly, Addie knew, faint, incoherent as she was, she knew. Hettie was stoppering the blood with her right arm, her fist—so much blood, all the sheets, every towel used—and pushing down hard with her other hand, leaning hard on Addie's uterus. He thought Hettie might be bruising her but Addie's face stayed calm, white, so white, tired, her eyes closed. And then Hettie started to nod, the bleeding had begun to clot, she said. Addie's eyes opened and she smiled, smiled as she lay her head back, and then, as if death might be easy, easier than watching Hettie pant, she closed her eyes the last time, tapped his hand. "Feeding will be hard," Addie whispered to him, "and the animals." She stayed breathing for a while after that, but the intervals grew longer. He waited, the whole of him poised for her next breath. And then— he was still waiting—Hettie held Addie's wrist for a moment, and turned away.

Someone else arrived. It was Josephine, with her applesauce cake. Addie had always liked Jo, liked how straight she spoke, how she fought to save the old schoolhouse. He could hear her in the kitchen now.

"Where's Willis? How is he?" She wouldn't whisper. No, she was marching in. "Willis!" Jo said, looking down on him, her hand on his shoulder. "You look like hell. Have you eaten anything?" He smiled and her eyes welled up. "How are we ever gonna get you through this?"

He looked away. He had seen that same face madder than hell and at him too, for doing nothing more than stopping to help her get her stalled car moving down the middle of River Street; she'd just learned to drive. Addie's face could sway like that too, from feeling to feeling, though hers, thank God, took a gentler swing.

They were all starting to come in now. He put down his knife and stood, watched as each one saw her in the corner, their faces breaking, turning away. It was her mouth mostly—all wrong—and her cheeks covered in face powder. He couldn't remember her ever wearing that. She looked more like herself when she was gray-white, dead white. But Lee Daunton wouldn't listen to him or to Hettie either. He said even men have to wear it after the embalming or they look too . . . "Dead?" Digger had asked. And then he had started laughing and couldn't stop. Every time he tried to stop, the word *dead* would come back to him. She would look like Addie, but she would look dead. It was more right to them that she didn't look like Addie. He couldn't stop laughing. Of course Mr. Daunton kept about his business, working the gravity pole and handing Sherm the jars of blood to put back in the bag. The boy had a knack for this work, his movements already graced by a discreet propriety. But he kept looking at Digger and later, out in the back, Digger heard his older brother, Freddie, explaining to him how he'd seen it before, the bereaved laughing like that. Deranged laughing, he said.

"Villis." It was Petra in her thick German accent, shaking her head and crossing herself. "May God keep you." She was still in her coat, her red-and-green-plaid scarf wrapped around her head and tied under her chin. She squeezed his arm. "Villis, you need clean for you, I clean." She stopped crossing herself and started scrubbing the air. "I scrub, I vash." He nodded.

Petra had said all that balderdash about them before they were married. "The sin of lust!" she'd said, shaking those same scrubbing, crossing fingers.

She gave him another squeeze. "You give message to my Karl, I come." Then she turned and left, crossing herself once more as she passed by Addie.

The women were talking—around him, then to him, one by one. Each face looked so kind but he was having trouble listening. Addie was becoming the dearest, the sweetest, a best friend, a very best friend, though Ruth, her truly best friend, had moved away over a month ago to live in her husband's hometown in Ohio, and Addie's sister, Edith, couldn't leave the farm two days in a row and she was bringing Leenie tomorrow. Edith was never comfortable around town folk anyway.

Doing the best I can, Addie. But he realized they could do it without him. They were talking mostly among themselves now.

Digger stepped into the backyard just as Jimmy's truck pulled up. Sometimes he arrived drunk but it didn't matter, Digger was grateful to him, as everyone was during times like these. Jimmy went to all the places Reverend Sims didn't, and he brought the corn liquor. Digger saw Elmer's dog in the back ready to jump out. Jimmy must've picked up Elmer in town.

Jimmy nodded as he approached, carrying his "medicine bag," a canvas bag strapped and buckled so the bottles didn't clink. He looked very serious. It was his moment of solemnity before he started doing his job, what he was known and appreciated for, which was being Jimmy: "We allowed in there? Or we gotta learn first how to be-have?"

Digger grinned. "I'm glad you've come."

Elmer stayed behind, his head down until Digger said hello to him. Elmer looked up sheepishly, caught Digger's eye, then lowered his head again. Elmer was a good cook and used to come early with the women, bringing a dish they would ooh and ah over, but it was always Addie he wanted to taste it, watching her face while she poked her spoon in and if she smiled, he would turn all red. But a couple of years back his spring dried up, and now one of the men usually brought him if he didn't smell too bad.

"Got some chairs in your shed, Willis? That's a fine place to be-have. What do *you* say, Elmer?" That was a joke because Elmer never said a word out loud. He had stopped speaking as a child, the day he started school. Sometimes he would write things down if you gave him paper and pen and it was, to him, a worthy question. Some kids that sneaked up on him at his parents' place said he spoke to his dog, E.D., for Elmer's Dog, because no one knew his real name. And just like Elmer, E.D. was welcome anywhere he turned up.

Jimmy found a chair with the back broken off in the corner of the woodshed, Elmer sat down on the chopping block, Digger turned a milk crate on end, and E.D. and Teddy stretched out on the dirt floor. The door opened from the kitchen and Josephine stepped over the dogs with a full plate of food. "Here you are, Willis, now you better eat." She handed him a fork and knife rolled up in a napkin. Then she saw Jimmy and added, "Even more reason. Nice to see you, Elmer. You want a plate?"

"We are be-havin', Josephine," Jimmy said. "Gonna bring *me* some food too?"

"Get it yourself. I take care of *nice* men."

"Ooohh, Josephine, the thought of heaven with you would send me off prayin'," he was grinning ear to ear, "prayin' to go to hell!" And he slapped his thigh and Josephine stuck her tongue out at him, though then she smiled at Digger. He couldn't help grinning. He felt safe in the shed.

More men were filing in. They knew Jimmy had arrived. Hettie came out with plates for Jimmy and Elmer and said to the others, "Come get your plates, boys. Get some food in you first." She had seen plenty of what happened when they didn't.

The men shook hands with Digger. Some said, *Sorry*. A few brought in some milk stools and a sawhorse from the barn, one sat on a stepladder. No one took off his coat but some laid their hats on their knees. Gradually, they went inside to pay their respects to Addie and came out with a plate. Everyone except Elmer and Jimmy. Jimmy never went in. That was the deal. And no one could tell what Elmer would do.

The talk started easy—about the price of feed. Ed Whittaker's grain bill was more than his milk check two months running. And the creamery boys got their pay cut too. When they started smoking, the talk went to the City. All those people and what is the one thing they need the most? Water. Some men with suits coming in last week, looking for a dam site. And more coming down from Albany too. Gonna flood the whole valley clear to Arena, one of them said, but some others didn't believe him. Jake was always talking doom and gloom, and how could you believe such a thing. Just mark my words, he said, sooner or later.

They never talked about Addie or the baby. They didn't need to, she was everywhere, in their faces, in their heavy movements, in their separate, lonely bodies passing the bottle. Digger got up and lit the lantern he kept by the door, hung it on the back wall. Every once in a while someone would step out and pee. Or someone would say, "What's that you got in your pocket, Elmer? A pickle?" And they'd all laugh. Elmer always carried his harmonica in his pocket, ever since his guitar got soaked in the last flood. Each time he'd laugh too, but he didn't take it out, not yet. He was on his own time.

And then one by one they left and each time, Addie's name rose up in their throats as they said the word *need*: "You need anything, Willis, just tell me . . ." "Now, you let me know . . ." "We'll be there if you need . . ." "You can count on us . . ." Elmer started playing to the men leaving. "Amazing Grace," his favorite. Most of the women who came with their neighbors left with their husbands, a few that lived close by walked home separately. Till only Josephine and Cynthia were left inside helping Hettie with the dishes.

Finally, Jimmy, not much drunker than when he came, stood up, leaned toward Digger, and whispered into his ear. "Elmer was cryin' for Addie when I found him, Will, he was bawlin' away." Digger nodded, and waited till Jimmy picked up his hat and his medicine bag to leave. Then, loud enough, he said, "Elmer, I'll take you back when I take Hettie and the baby." Elmer nodded and kept playing. "Swing Low, Sweet Chariot." Digger could hear the women singing in the kitchen, *Coming for to carry me home*, every time it came around, and it kept coming, each time a little different, another note stretched or cut short, rising or wailing. Digger closed his eyes and fell into the sound, as if he were swimming through the darkness, the notes like a string of buoys lifting him from one to the next and the next.

Finally Digger stood up and said, "Come inside, Elmer, play a few songs for Addie."

After everyone was gone, it took a while for Digger to rub all the coloring off Addie's face. He ran his rough hand over her dress, her wedding dress, cream colored and lacy. It gapped open on the left side by her ribs, too tight now to button all the way down the back. But Hettie had been sure, so sure that this was the dress Addie should wear. He didn't argue.

Four and a half years earlier he had stood at the back of the town hall with the justice of the peace and watched Addie come in, a little clumsily, holding a handful of black-eyed Susans. When he saw Hettie prepare Addie's body, washing, washing away the blood, the bucket of water growing pink, then red and brown, he became a stranger, not only to her, but also to the table and chairs, to the cupboard, to the sink and faucet as he filled another bucket.

The dress was more alive now than she was. He would take it off to bury her. *For naked we shall return,* especially she who loved nakedness, recognized it everywhere. Once she told him he was most naked in his nightshirt. He lifted her out of the casket and set her on the sheet he had laid on the table, the sheet he would wrap her in. How could her body be so cold? Like stone or iron. He raised her torso from the back of her neck, undid the top button, then the second and third down. Strands of hair from her braid caught in his hands, tangled in the buttons. He had hurried, again, like that night he had scared her.

Not their wedding night, but their first night, a stolen night they had painstakingly arranged. She had stood in the rented room, her thigh brushing against the bedspread, and he had rushed, his hands too large, his fingers thumbs. He felt her retreat and he panicked, rushing, wanting more. "Stop!" she yelled, and frightened by his own urgency, he couldn't come near her again for weeks.

Now with each button he unbuttoned, her body came closer, so close, yet no longer his.

He laid her slowly down, but her right arm slapped against the table and slipped off. He lifted her arm back on, but then her left foot and calf fell off the other side. He smiled. She was playing with him, wasn't she? She would do that, make him grin, bring him out of his *gloom*. "Thy very sublime gloom," she'd tease.

He lowered the dress and laid it on the chair. He unfolded the ends of the diaper, pulled it and the toweling gently away. He turned his face, the smell of birth and death overpowering. And still some blood, dried there in that place that used to pull him toward itself—from out in the barn, in the orchard, across the fields, that place where he had come to learn the carefulness of love, its tender, unrelenting heat. He paused now, looked at her, her limbs disheveled. He could not wrap the sheet around her right away. He began to arrange her, and as he did, her body became slowly, carefully naked and forgave him everything.

3

Leenie and her ma knocked on Willis's back door, hollered, walked into the woodshed, hollered. Waited, hollered. No sound. And no sign of the dog, Teddy. Piles of split wood, kindling mostly, on either side of the chopping block, Willis's ax thrown on the ground. A few empty liquor bottles by some milk crates, a broken chair, a jug of hard cider on the bench near the wall. Leenie followed her ma into the kitchen, holding back, like she used to when she walked into church, thinking *God's house.* This was different, more quiet, but the same feeling of holy, *the house of the dead.*

The kitchen didn't smell. It used to hit Leenie first thing when they'd visit, the bread baking, meat roasting, onions or potatoes or squash, smells that she imagined always surrounded Addie, even when she was outside hoeing or hanging the wash. Mama waved her hand over the stove, touched the pot on the back burner.

"Cold as stone!" she said like a curse. She lifted the lid, peered in. "Must be Cynthia Jenkins brought her pea soup."

Leenie saw through the doorway into the parlor. That's the room, she thought. She followed her mother, but then held back again, readying herself to face where she knew the coffin would be, kitty-corner against the wall. And there it was—under a wreath of princess pine. But it was empty. Neither of them moved. As if the emptiness took a while to cross the room so that they understood Addie wasn't there. And then they saw the dress. Mama let out a noise—a night sound, half cry, half scream, like a cat's. She started to run, and Leenie ran too, past the fancy sofa and up the stairs, into one, two, three bedrooms, into Addie's sewing room, knowing again, as each door banged open, Addie was gone.

Mama ran outside and across the yard to the cow barn. Leenie watched her from the kitchen window. She wanted to stay in the house, it was quieter than any house she'd ever been in. She stared out the window a long time, like she was staring at nothing. But then what was nothing became the something right in front of her, the main barn, and smack up against it, Frances's favorite tree, a soft maple, leafless now. Every time they'd been here, Uncle Willis threatened to cut that tree down, probably just to hear Frances howl and Addie laugh and say, "Over my dead body." And then she'd turn to Frances sitting next to her and touch her hand. "Don't you worry, dear," like they were fellow champions of that tree.

Leenie walked out toward the back of the barn, in by the new heifer pen, through the milk room, but there was no Mama, no Uncle Willis, not even his dog. She hurried out the south side by the silo and toward the stable where the two workhorses, Dan and Johnny, were kept at night. In front of their stalls, a couple chickens scratched at some feed dropped from the horses' mouths. "Mama?" she said, and though she didn't hear anything, she stepped into the back where the harnesses and rigs hung in the dark and a feed bin lined the wall, giving off the smell of molasses and oats.

She heard sniffling behind her. She turned and stared into the dark until her mother took shape. She was sitting on a storage trunk, crying.

"Go on," Mama said, waving her arm, "I'm alright."

Leenie walked toward her. "I'll just set here. I'll just set with you." She didn't say, "I love you, Ma." She didn't touch her shoulder. It was all she could do to listen to her mother cry as she stared at a barn cat sleeping in the corner on a pile of moldy hay.

Finally her ma stopped crying and started swallowing and holding her elbows. "Leenie," her voice was flat, cold. "I seen what you done to the mare."

Leenie stiffened.

"How you think we're gonna get through next fall, huh? Tryin' to work a mare nine, ten months on. And foalin' when it's near winter, you thought of that? With only the straight stalls we got. What did you think, Leenie, the foal was gonna arrive in a great big box stall like at Charlie Owen's?"

Leenie ran her hand back and forth along the cold metal frame of the trunk while her ma kept talking straight ahead into the air.

"And what are we gonna do then? With a new mouth to feed. And who's gonna train it? Who's got time to train some foal, some *thoroughbred* foal? Won't be any use for three, four years, if then." She threw up her hand. "And all the time eatin'."

Leenie started rocking.

"But you think about that? No, you're just dreamin' on Charlie Owen's line. You can have your high-falutin' dreams, Leenie, but you leave me, you leave us and our life out of 'em, you hear? You hear me?"

Leenie did, but it wasn't a real question. She knew her ma was finished, and when she was finished, there wasn't another word could be said about it.

After a long while, Leenie stood up and said, "I gotta pee." Her ma didn't move. Leenie wanted to hate her, but she couldn't. She had it in her—she called it her stone hate, it was always there, low in her chest and ready. But after hearing her ma cry and looking down on her dark hair, her shoulders narrow and hunched, she looked too small. She wasn't Norwegian blood, like the rest of them. And there was something else, a thought that rode in underneath: she could die, her mother. It made Leenie want to run.

Coming into the light, she saw cows grazing on the far slope above the river and in the small front pasture where the sun was still shining, the horses, Dan and Johnny, facing each other, their necks side by side and their heads tilted, licking each other's withers. *The easy side of November.* But the words came with tears—back behind her eyes where Mary always held them. Nothing was easy with Mama, ever. And how stupid, a winter foal. To think it could've pleased her.

She sat in the outhouse a long time, the way you can once the ground freezes but it's not too cold. It seemed just the right size for a house and dark enough too. The two holes made her remember again why they were here. How they always said AddieandWillis like they were one. She leaned forward and held herself. She wanted to stay there forever, but outside on the hill behind her, Teddy, Uncle Willis's dog, was barking.

Coming out, she saw something red move in the woods. The red came closer, and it was her uncle in a red shirt coming down from the hollow, what he always called his wasteland. She should go get her mama, she thought, but she didn't, she waited behind the old lilac. Teddy ran out of the woods in front of her uncle, but then stuck right on his heel as they crossed the yard and headed into the house.

Mama came from the barn then too, walking fast. Leenie followed her in through the back door.

Uncle Willis turned around from the sink. He had the wildest look Leenie ever saw in a man's eye, even wilder than the man singing at the revival by the school, his eyes crawling back into his head like he was looking there for where the Lord lives. But this wild was not a looking for the Lord, it was the woods, and it was death, it was Aunt Addie missing.

Mama said sharply, "Where is she? You told me they wouldn't take her till this evenin.'" Leenie shot her a glance. Was her ma looking at him? She was, but maybe she wasn't seeing him because then she asked when the burial would be.

"Ain't gonna be one, not a church burial," Uncle Willis said in a far-off voice that matched his eyes, wiping his hands on the side of his pants.

"Willis John!"

"I'm not Willis anymore. Call me Digger."

"Digger? Now, don't you go off crazy now, Willis. You got a baby. Hettie Brower can't keep keepin' her. And my daughter's here. Just like we agreed. The stove's cold. She's gotta eat food. Hot food, you hear? And my sister's gonna have her burial, her church burial."

He shook his head.

Mama looked him up, down—he was a tall man, and thin, but with a farmer's shoulders. She paused over his face like she was reading in bad light. Then all of a sudden, she rushed past the table and hit him on the chest with both fists.

He just stood there, his back to the sink, like a tree trunk when there isn't a wind but it's cold. Mama hit him as hard as she could. Again and again. Finally, he caught her two hands.

She started snarling. "You better do right by my sister in her death or by God, I am goin' . . ." The muscles in her arms kept tightening as Willis held her hands still. He looked like the calm one now.

Then he started preaching. Leenie should've known he would because she had seen that calm before. Uncle Willis would stand up before a holiday supper—Thanksgiving, Christmas, Easter—and wait till they hushed before he spoke.

"The Lord hath said, an altar of earth thou shalt make." Willis let Ma's hands go.

Mama sat down at the table like she was wilted. She might've asked *what,* but he would've repeated it even if she hadn't. He always repeated what came from the Bible.

"But if thou lift up thy tool upon it, thou hast desecrated . . ." He said it over and over.

Ma's voice was weak. "Desecrate?"

He nodded. "Your sister's stone will not be marked, Edith." His voice dropped, it felt soothing to Leenie. "It will endure. Pure and clean, untouched by all save weather, save God the Father. Free even from the ravages of the river."

"But her name . . ."

"No tool," he answered.

She asked again, "Her name?"

"No tool," he repeated, shaking his head.

"But that means—" She didn't finish. They were silent, Mama at the table with her head in her hands. After a long while, the silence became more than no talking, the way cold becomes more than no heat. Cold holding tight to the valley floor in what they called inversion. The silence of death was inversion too.

"You buried her, didn't you. Tell me where she is, Willis."

He leaned back against the sink, staring down at Mama, not saying a word. His eyes had grown calm again.

"It ain't time yet!" Ma hit the table with her fist.

He didn't answer and she didn't wait. She stood up, grabbed Leenie's arm. "Come on. Ain't a fit place for you."

Leenie stood against the doorjamb to the dining room. "No, Mama."

But her mama didn't hear, she kept yanking at her. Finally she stopped, fixed her eyes on her daughter, her face turning more and more confused as it became clear that Leenie was not going with her. Her child was not going with her.

4

Teddy barked at the wheels of Osmer's Model T, but Digger didn't bother to call him, damn dog never learned anyway. He waited by Leenie's trunk while Teddy chased the car halfway to the Stones' place before heading back, wagging his tail like he'd done a good thing.

It was turning cold, but Digger could still smell the river. It hadn't frozen yet and it was low, down to the mudflats. As a boy, when the water dropped this low he'd roll his wagon down to the mud and spend a morning getting it stuck and pulling it out like he was three or four men. A few times the wheels sunk in so deep, he had to run to the barn and get a shovel. It never did turn to work, though—in that silt, a shovel seemed to dig of its own accord. The river smell always brought him some relief. As if his soul, like the East Branch, reached all the way up to the headwaters in Grand Gorge, and downriver too, through Peaceful Valley and into Shinhopple until just west of Fish's Eddy, where it gave itself to the Delaware. There, at the junction, he seemed to end.

As soon as he opened the door, he realized how cold it had gotten in the kitchen. "If you're cold, put on a coat," he said as he set the trunk down by the door to the parlor. Leenie was reading at the table. Like she did whenever the family came for holidays.

She would poke through Addie's bookcase and plunk down in the parlor till someone dragged her out, usually her mother.

"If you're cold, put on a coat," he said again and Leenie looked up, her face far away, but open. She was Sam's daughter alright, with her broad jaw and stringy blond hair, though it was pulled into a ponytail. Not at all like her mother, staring at him over the hood of the car just now with those dark eyes set close, saying, "I'm gonna watch you, Willis John."

He lit two lamps behind the cookstove, rolled the wicks down, and set a lamp on the table. "Ain't good for your eyes to read in the dark," he said and stepped into the woodshed.

There was just enough gray light coming in the windows. He found his small ax in the corner and split some hemlock he wanted to get rid of—almost worthless, but good enough for the fall. He saved the hardwood for the dead of winter. He carried a load back to the stove, closed the kitchen door behind him, pulled up his stool. No coals left in the firebox, just ash to shovel out. He'd have to start over.

"Want to spread this ash on the vegetable garden?" He heard the chair scrape and handed Leenie the ash bucket as she crossed in front of the light. "Throw it just this side of the rasp-berries. You'll still be able to see." Addie and he'd be bickering now—she'd want it around her lilacs, he'd want it for the garden.

He watched Leenie as she left, her sweater a dark gray, stained or faded he couldn't tell. Wondered if her dress—a dark thing too—was one that Addie gave her. She'd always find clothes in town for them at the rummage sales. "At least something those girls can wear," she'd say, "and not look like urchins."

He picked the top *Valley Gazette* from the stack of old papers by the kindling box, noticed the date, October 18—how many days was that before? There was so much hope then, so much *expectancy*. The only bad news the mention of some City boys poking around the East Branch, some like Jake saying they're on the hunt for a dam site. Digger rolled up the paper, threw the wads in the firebox. Picked from the pile of kindling a few shingles he'd ripped off the roof of the chicken coop—they'd light up good and quick. He propped them against the paper, put a couple skinnier sticks of hemlock on top, lit it, watched it catch before he closed the door.

"Louise Campbell has loads of milk," Hettie had said as she started clearing mucus from the baby's mouth. "We need to get her there. I'll bring her back as soon as you get help." That's the first he'd thought of Leenie, he never paid her much attention before. She was the quieter one, smart as a whip but quiet. Not like Frances—a ball of fire everyone loved, fire, but spit too. "I have an idea," he had said to Edith the night she came to sit watch. As he spoke, she looked straight at him, as if every word got handled some, sifted before she'd let it settle. She nodded slowly at first, then almost smiled, like he was the answer to a question she'd had for a long time.

Leenie walked back in, shivering, set the ash bucket down next to him before she sat back down in the chair, Addie's chair. She looked too lean. "Cold, put on a coat," he said. But she just sat there, the spitting image of her pa. He liked Sam alright, though he drank too much, liked how smart he was—just wasn't meant for a farm, that's all, though it was hard to say what he was meant for, if it wasn't to charm women, except of course his wife. Addie always stuck up for him. But he was a seed that wouldn't set deep in the soil. And his poor children were proof.

Maybe she doesn't *have* a coat. But he didn't say anything. It was late and he had to milk and feed yet. First Teddy. "Come here, boy." He scooped a ladle of cold, thick soup into the dog dish—not much left and the thought of eating it made him sick, like most food did now.

The barn might give him a reprieve. But then he scoffed at himself for the thought. As if there were places God's voice didn't reach. But never mind Him, he had to get out. This was *her* house, *her* kitchen, but it was *his* barn. He lit the lantern he kept by the door. "Keep the stove goin', hear?" He waited a moment for Leenie to nod and stepped into the shed.

A wave of light fell on Addie's red woolen coat, her garden coat. He stopped. He'd been walking by it all day but this was the first he saw it, hanging on the clothes pole. He put the lantern down. It had been her fancy coat till moths ate holes in the wool, and now most the lining was torn too. He touched the sleeve; it was so infused with her, so close, he thought he was about to faint, but instead he reached out and lifted it off the hook—as if he were someone else, someone who knew how to keep his arms and legs moving. He was walking back up the steps, opening the kitchen door, he was standing at the table holding a coat over the light. Who was he, handing over to this girl his wife's dirty coat? She lifted her head, looked at him, then at the coat. Then she stood up and took it and suddenly he felt full of relief, even love. For Leenie being there. For Leenie being cold and needing the coat, taking the coat. He turned quickly and walked out. He couldn't bear to see her put it on.

Digger saw a light inside the barn, shifting from one window to the next. Burdett, his hired man, was moving a lantern—it was just like him to start in without a word, he could come and go without Teddy even barking. Digger pulled the door back and saw the lanterns hanging halfway down the litter aisle. They'd be done in less than an hour.

He nodded to Burdett on his way to the milk room, where the lamp threw enough light in the doorway that he could find a clean pail in front of the sink. And he could see Burdett had replenished the straw in the calf pen. He grabbed his stool off the wall of the feed alley and set that and his pail under Jane, the next cow in line. Burdett, on his way to the other side, handed him a bucket of soapy water. As he swung into the old routine, Digger felt some relief, surrounded by his Jerseys and the low, close ceiling, the beams needing another coat of whitewash. He cleaned Jane off and dried her, then felt between her udder and back legs. She'd been chapped badly enough to bleed there, but the petrolatum had softened it, it didn't even feel red. He pulled on one of her teats and started stripping.

Burdett hummed as they moved from one cow to the next, sharing the bucket of water. Occasionally a cow swatted one of them in the face with her tail. Burdett would only grunt but Digger would curse before he stuck the tail under his knee and continued on, emptying the pails of milk into the cans that they rolled down the aisle into the milk room.

He was a good worker, Burdett, and the cows and horses took to him. He'd been Digger's hired man a few hours a day, sometimes more, sometimes less, since he dropped out of school maybe ten years back.

It wasn't till Burdett had set his last can in the water vat and Digger had started on Belle, his last cow, a stripper almost dry, that he saw Leenie standing by the stanchion, watching him. In Addie's coat.

"Get back in the house."

She didn't move.

"Back in the house," he yelled louder, before she turned and disappeared from the light.

A cat yowled from the crawl space below, and Digger dropped his head onto Belle's side, leaned his forehead into her ribs. The grief would rise up on its own like a flood and take him, sudden yet slow moving, too slow. Why didn't he drown? He wanted to drown. *All the night make I my bed to swim; I water my couch with tears.* Tonight might be the longest yet.

He surfaced again, numb. Finished her off, a little more than half a bucket, not bad for a stripper—maybe she would last into winter. He poured her milk into the can, rolled it to the milk room to cool in the water. Five cans for the night. He left Burdett to hay in the horses, hunt down the last of the chickens that hadn't made it back to the coop.

Digger knew what he had to do; it had been dark over an hour, Hettie wasn't going to make it there, and in the morning who could guess who'd give her a ride or just come by to check on him or give him food. They'd see the casket, start talking, at Lloyd's, or worse, at church. Soon Reverend Sims would find out. Digger took a lantern into his toolshed to find a saw and his go-devil, or his sledge, it didn't matter. The toolshed was filled mostly with what needed fixing, boxes of cutter and plough parts, wheels, fencing, an old clock, a scale missing its weights. He smelled the stale gasoline from one of the cans he kept by the door. In a heap of tools, he found the go-devil. But his saws were hung up on the far wall behind some broken chairs. Most of them needed sharpening, except his bucksaw, he could use his bucksaw.

As soon as he stepped out with his tools, he saw the barn was dark, Burdett had headed home. The north ridge loomed up black behind the catalpa his mother planted, its branches spread upon the hill, Addie's hill now. She had loved that catalpa, loved its leaves, big and heart shaped. He turned and walked down the path worn in the grass toward the small glimmer in the kitchen.

Leenie was reading again by the table lamp. He was used to her there, but he hadn't been ready to see her in the barn, he saw the red coat and . . . he'd spoken harshly. "I'll take your trunk upstairs," he said as gently as he could. She didn't move, or speak, even when he came back down. "First room on the left if you want to go to bed." Then he explained, "Hettie, she doesn't like to travel in the dark if she doesn't have to." Leenie nodded but didn't look up from her book. He wanted to yell out, but what could he say? Nothing. Addie would have made her feel welcome, but as it was, the silence and darkness snuffed out any life left in the house.

He lit a lamp in the parlor and the light spread in an oval over Addie's bookcase and his mother's gold overstuffed chair, and the corner where the casket was. He lifted an end off the gurney. It wasn't as heavy as he figured. The two of them could manage it—if she could balance it, he'd bear most the weight.

"You gotta help me here, Leenie."

"Alright," she said softly and kept reading.

He waited, looking aimlessly at the wallpaper, stripes of green lacy leaves on a background of gold. "Well, you gonna just set there?"

She put down her book. "Not if you tell me what to do. I thought you meant help as in . . . abstract help."

"Abstract help! Now, doesn't that beat all, *abstract* help. No, Miss Leenie, I simply need help liftin' this."

She was a tall girl, a lot taller than Addie, though the coat fit her well enough, her shoulders filled it out and she didn't look so skinny, or cold. She approached slowly, looking at the casket.

"We gotta get it to the woodshed. You take that end."

She nodded and the casket rose up between them.

"Stronger'n you look."

"You too," she answered, her face staying relaxed as they carried it. He kicked open the door to the shed, and they lowered it down the steps and set it on the floor in front of the chopping block. She stood back, waited a moment, then turned to leave. "Shut the door," he said. "And I don't mean an *abstract door.*"

She glanced back and smiled a broad, unexpected smile and then stepped into the kitchen.

He looked down at the casket. He'd told Lee Daunton he didn't need any plot, he'd bury Addie himself on his own land. The law said nothing about that, it only specified a casket as necessary. It was a wrong law but it didn't bother Digger, it wasn't the law's province to know the words of the Lord: *Naked ye shall return . . . from dust ye return to dust.* He'd just go about his business, and as Jimmy always said, what the law doesn't know, doesn't hurt it. It was Sims who bothered him—if *he* found out Addie was buried in a sheet, he'd drive straight to the town hall, so cocksure his Church had been violated. But in spring Addie loved to sink her hands in the soil just as soon as it thawed. She was so thoroughly comfortable with the ground that for a moment here and there when he didn't ache too badly, he could feel she was just returning home.

He opened the casket, and saw blood on the satin lining. He let the lid drop.

He felt under the bench against the wall, and found a bottle of Jimmy's liquor. He took a long pull but it didn't help. He took another, and another. She's not in it, he kept saying to himself. He took another swallow, and another. The cold of the dirt floor was seeping in through the soles of his shoes. *Mine eye is consumed because of grief; it waxeth old.* "It waxeth old," he yelled, "but Thou, O Lord, how long?"

He looked up. Leenie stood in the doorway. He couldn't see her face.

"Don't let the heat out," he said, and swallowed.

"What heat?" Leenie asked.

He raised the bottle and laughed. "This heat." The liquor was going down easy.

"What are you gonna do?" She nodded toward the casket.

"I'm gonna smash it. Saw it up to burn." She stepped down onto the dirt.

"It's too cold in here for you," he said. She walked toward him, and he saw the frayed lining of the coat sleeve.

"Give it here," she said. "Come on, give it here."

"The go-devil?" He started laughing again. "Or the heat? You want the heat?"

"The go-devil," she said softly. "Give it."

"First you gotta have some heat!" He raised the bottle again, and she grabbed it. She brought it to her lips and tipped it back.

"Just like your daddy."

She handed the bottle back and opened her hand. "Come on, give me the go-devil. Give it here."

Her hand stayed there, waiting.

"What do *you* know about death?"

"Nothin."

"Damn right. Nothin."

"Nothin," she repeated as her hand closed around the wood above his hand, and he let her take it.

"Nothin'! You don't know nothin'!" he said.

She stood back from the box and the coat widened before him as she spread her feet. She gripped the handle with both hands.

"Even the Daunton boy, the youngest, he knows how—"

"Tell me when you're ready." She raised the go-devil up above her shoulder. How long could she hold it in the air? He watched its shadow shake on the far wall.

"Now!" he yelled.

The ax head split open the top of the box, a piece hit his leg, his chest. He jumped up. "Again!" The box bounced as she lifted the go-devil back up through the wood and down hard.

"Again! Again!" Each hit, more joints gave, the wood broke and flew apart, hit the ground, the wall. He kept yelling, though he couldn't hear himself as the box bounced, shattered on the dirt.

"Stop!" he shouted, falling back onto his seat. "Stop. Stop." He took a swig. "Stop." The go-devil rested motionless by her side. The night too, motionless. No cats howling, no rabbits, not even an owl.

"It's over," he squeezed his eyes shut. "Now get out."

She leaned the handle against his leg, then walked to the woodpile and picked up a piece of maple.

"That's the hardwood," he said.

"I know." And she picked up two more.

"You cook?"

"At home," she said and carried the wood up the steps into the kitchen.

5

Leenie threw the covers back, stepped into the cold, and dressed as fast as she could. Frost-hills peaked halfway up the inside of the windows (what Mary and Janey still called fairy mountains). She was very hungry. And she wasn't going to eat that pea soup left in the pot again. This morning, she said to herself, in her home voice, not her school voice, you ain't gonna filch food from the dog, you're gonna cook yourself a feast. She put on the coat Uncle Willis had given her last night. How many times did he say it, "Put on a coat," while she sat there holding her tongue. That she didn't even own one was *not* going to be the first thing he was to learn about her. Then she'd have to hear again about her wretched pa, though now her uncle was sleeping off a drunk too, snoring across the hall.

She made the bed, thinking how Addie used to keep the house so tidy—the bedside table with its tatted doily, the pillowcase embroidered in yellow and green to match the yellow curtains and green quilt. She plumped up the two pillows, such a big bed and she was in it all alone, she'd never slept alone before.

Leenie picked up the chamber pot she'd used during the night and carried it downstairs and outdoors. It was snowing lightly but it hadn't stuck to the ground yet, except up on the north ridge. The snow line was horizontal and created a bright rectangle between the gray sky and the darker, lower fields. Suddenly she saw rectangles everywhere standing out against the frost: the barn, the milk room, the stable, the chicken coop, the smokehouse, the toolshed and the little barn, the outhouse where she dumped the pot, all the doors and windows. And there were triangles too, from the gables and slopes.

Geometry. So peaceful, she thought. Or maybe it was that everything was well tended, painted a new deep red (except the barn wall where the soft maple grew). Her uncles always chortled over her pa not using paint, like it was his choice. "Smart-come-to-nothin'," even Aunt Addie would say when Mama left the room. As if Leenie and her sisters didn't have ears. "Losing not one, but two farms and a river farm to boot!" Leenie walked back indoors and rinsed out the pot in the kitchen sink. *Running water.* Just-like-that and a tiny dam lets loose and just-like-that it stops. It sure wouldn't be hard getting used to that.

First, she had to get the stove going. The fire was almost out, only a few coals left. She was about to shovel them together when she saw something whitish in the back and reached in. Ashes flew everywhere, floated in the air before they snowed down, onto her and onto the piece she lifted out, a piece of satin, cream colored, shiny, only its edges curled and blackened. Leenie smoothed it across her lap. It was Addie's dress, her wedding dress. There was still lace from around the neck and three tiny buttonholes. She traced them with her fingers. She shut her eyes and sat petting the satin while the kitchen got colder. *He had burned her dress.* Did he just stuff it in the stove? Most the night he'd been yelling psalms, and later, near morning, she heard him crying in his bedroom, and then he started to snore. She'd never seen such grief. Her mother's was old and stale, from the hardness of her life. His burned in the air.

She shivered and put the piece of dress in her pocket. She scraped the coals and went to the shed for kindling. The empty bottle lay on the dirt by the chopping block. Splintered boards were everywhere, and the lining from the casket lay shredded. Hettie was coming with the baby, but Leenie wasn't going to clean up the mess, that was *his* job. She picked up some kindling and hurried out. She'd better wake him.

As soon as the kindling caught, she headed upstairs, slipped the piece of Addie's dress into her trunk, and turned back into the hall. But there, standing in front of his bedroom door, she froze. She'd been hearing his snoring all morning but now it was too close, rising and breaking like the psalms he shouted.

Finally, she turned the knob and entered. The room was big, the bed a four-poster. Uncle Willis lay on his back, a quilt and wool blanket pulled partway up his chest. His mouth was open so she could see his teeth, yellow and old, and the small hairs in his nose quivered with each snore. Above the neck of his union suit, his skin was reddish brown where the sun hit, pinky white where it didn't. She touched her finger to the deepest wrinkle in his forehead. She was not frightened of him, not frightened at all.

Uncle Willis was awake, she'd made sure of that, yelling in his ear and shaking him, but he'd be more inclined to come down, she figured, when he smelled breakfast. She lit a lantern and went down to the cellar. She raised the light and saw the shelves filled with what Addie canned last summer. Tomatoes, string beans, lima beans, corn, cauliflower, peas, jellies, watermelon rinds, pickles. And there were baskets of potatoes, white and red, and the little pig potatoes you could eat in one bite. And garlic, onions, apples. Not apples as hard as theirs, though, that's one thing her family had—apples that stayed tart till Christmas.

The spring box was in the corner. Under the water, she saw just one jar of milk. On the shelf against the box was the same sourdough culture she'd grown up with that came from her great-aunt—a famous spy in the Civil War—and two tubs of butter, what looked like a jug of cider, a big tub of pot cheese, and head cheese she hated and never had to eat because her daddy hated it too. Only called it cheese he said, try to fool children can't be fooled. And then on the shelf up above the waterline where it wasn't as cold, an opened jar of pickles, Addie's bread-and-butter pickles. Her favorite. Leenie screwed off the lid, pinched out some with her fingers, and shoved them into her mouth, she couldn't help herself, the little rounds loaded with mustard seed and skinny strings from the onions, so sweet they burned. She stood there chewing every one till there was nothing left to chew, right down to the last pickle. She could hear Addie repeating to her mother, "It's the cassia buds make it." And Mama nodding, but she didn't grow cassia so that was that.

She put the jar back on the shelf, though it was nothing now but juice and seeds, dipped her hands in the spring box to wash off the stickiness. Slabs of bacon hung from the beams, and sausages the Polish man in town made, the skins white with mold. And two hams strung up by the door to the root cellar—more food than she'd seen in years and Uncle Willis still had a pig left to kill. She wanted more than anything in the world a real breakfast—bacon, eggs, bread, coffee. Like *normal*—a word she loved. She lowered a slab of bacon from the beam and carried it up the stairs.

By the time Digger came down, she'd already made coffee. Bacon grease was splattering and smelling so good it was all she could do not to burn her fingers stealing crispies. Digger was wearing one of his red-checkered barn caps pulled so low you could barely see his face. He took a cup off the shelf and poured himself coffee. She could smell him as he came near, whiskey, wood smoke, something sour. He walked over to the sink and stared out the window. Finally he took a sip and like a dry heave hit him, spit it out.

"Don't make this much, do ya?"

"It's Ma always makes it."

He was swallowing, grimacing. Like Janey eating a tomato.

"You want a couple eggs?" she asked, turning the bacon in the middle of the pan. "I saw what you got in the cellar and *I* am gonna eat, I'm gonna eat well."

"If you eat, you won't talk." Then he eyed her, her or the coat, she couldn't tell. "Better if you don't talk."

She hit an egg hard onto the side of the pan, cracking the shell clean, then another, one two three four eggs. She felt the air over the back burners and decided on the one farthest right. She didn't like her eggs cooked too hot. And I don't like *him* much neither, she thought, before she corrected herself in her mind: *either,* don't like him either. It was when she got riled. Addie used to say it, anger and grammar don't sit well together, though Leenie never heard Addie speak badly, not like Leenie's mama, who was nine years older and had to leave school for work when she turned ten.

She looked at him. "It's you who better eat. Food'll soak up some of that whiskey." Riding the drink down, her daddy called it. She opened up the warmer on the top of the stove, put in the bread she'd cut and watered—Addie's bread, probably a week old.

Digger poured himself more coffee. "And it ain't a bad idea to filter out the grounds," he said and sat down in front of the silverware she had set out.

She served up his eggs and bread and bacon, figuring he liked his bacon the way her daddy did—"still young." But then at the table, she stalled.

"You don't take your hat off when you eat?"

He didn't answer or look at her or move. She waited, holding the plate up in the air till finally he set his hat beside him and she gave him his breakfast.

She ate too, and neither of them said a word. Like cows, she thought, tethered in their stanchions, chewing. She felt again the heaviness, the air thick with it, and no girls to crack it with their chattering, no Janey, no Mary, no Frances laughing or squealing, no little Emma. She wished more than anything to be home.

When he finished, he pushed the empty plate away and licked his teeth clean while he looked at her, his eyes softer now. So there he is, she thought, coming out of hiding. But then just as quickly, he slipped back, he was gone.

"You're a long way in there, ain't ya, Uncle Willis?"

He didn't look away and she knew she was being studied. She didn't look away either, she was waiting for him to answer.

"Yut," he finally said and nodded.

"Your head feel any better?" She was sucking on the bacon rinds, they'd break your teeth if you chewed them.

"Nope," he said and stood.

"It will." She felt old enough now, now that her stomach was full. "I didn't grow up with my daddy for nothin'."

He looked down and smiled. It took her thoroughly by surprise.

Leenie had finished washing the china and was wiping the bacon pan with newspaper when she saw the green coat through the sink window, a few flakes of snow on the shoulders. Hettie Brower was walking toward the back door. Leenie had heard stories about her from the time she was young, mostly that

Hettie helped out girls hell-bent on ruining the men in town, but the strangest story of all was that she lived alone and was known to like it that way. Well, here goes, Leenie said to herself, wiping off her hands. You've taken care of babies plenty— Emma, Janey, even Mary as soon as you were big enough to hold her.

Hettie stepped into the kitchen from the shed. She looked so small up close—Leenie had only seen her from the car when she was walking on the road. She stared at Leenie and took a deep breath. "So, you're Edith's oldest." Her face was long and thin with a long, straight nose and high cheekbones, full of hundreds of wrinkles. Leenie had never seen anything like them—they were very, very fine, like hair painstakingly combed in different-size swirls.

"My name's Leenie."

"Leenie. Well, you're a grown girl now, ain't ya?" Hettie smiled.

She must have been very beautiful once, Leenie thought as Hettie crossed the kitchen toward the stove, the baby wrapped in a gray blanket against her chest and shoulder. Hettie's gait made her seem young, as if she'd been born with all those wrinkles. She waved her free hand over the burners.

"Warm in here. That's good."

Leenie nodded. Addie's casket was still burning, the last of what Uncle Willis had just finished picking up. Hettie looked around. "Where is he?"

Leenie pointed her head toward the barn, and then glanced again at the baby.

"A sleepy li'l girl," Hettie said and handed her over. "But with no name yet."

Leenie opened the top of the blanket and looked in. She didn't look like Addie at all, or Willis either. Asleep, she looked

Oriental, and maybe too, like Wade, Leenie's little brother born between Mary and Janey. He lived only ten days and no one ever knew why he died.

Leenie had never been a coochee-coo person. She sat down on the rocker next to the stove and placed her finger on the baby's lips. The baby started sucking right away—Leenie didn't even have to prod. "You're a pretty one, ain't ya?" she said in her home voice. "And a good strong suck to you too."

"They had a few names for boys—Robert, John, William— but none for a girl. It was your ma, they thought, would have all the girls." Hettie got a pot off the rack and filled it with water at the sink. "I brought only one bottle of Louise's milk. Richard's bringing more from her when he comes through on his route. And I found a few extra bottles for you to use. Guess Addie never imagined she'd be needing *them.* And I guess she don't need 'em now, does she? She don't need nothin' now." Hettie seemed very old suddenly, staring out at the barn, at the arcs scratched in from the maple. "Did your mother talk to you about nursin', dry nursin'?"

Leenie stiffened. "No."

The baby stopped sucking and started to fuss, making crying noises. Leenie rubbed her finger softly on her lips, pushing in just slightly, tapping; the baby squinched her mouth into an O but still wouldn't suck.

Hettie carried the pan to the stove, took the bottle from her coat pocket, set it in the water, and without even feeling where the heat was, pushed the pan back and off to the right.

She knows *this* stove, Leenie thought and wondered how many houses she'd not only been inside, but a part of too.

"Make it easier in the long run. And you just might get some milk comin' in, and though it'll never be much, it'll make a difference tryin' to console her."

Leenie brought the baby to her chest, patted her back but she wouldn't stop fussing.

"And it's good you ain't wearin' a dress—shirts and skirts from now on." She was coming toward Leenie. "Here, lean forward, I'll undo your brassiere. Don't worry, it ain't nothin' to be scared of."

Leenie folded forward over the baby, who was still fussing. She figured Hettie would find out for herself.

"Now, what in heaven's?" Hettie sputtered.

Leenie pulled her lips in tight. She wasn't wearing a normal brassiere, the kind you buy. At first Leenie had been happy her breasts were starting to show, she'd hold them at night. Like two countries, she imagined them, separate principalities with their own rivers and hills that she would follow up and down and around with her fingers. She was twelve, thirteen maybe, but then they kept growing and she started to hate them, refusing to go back to school in the fall for her last year. But before September came, her ma had made what she called a binder from feed sacks sewn into the belly of an old corset with eyelets all along the front and laces Leenie could pull tight till she looked almost flat again, like her sisters. And though Frances was getting breasts now too, it didn't make Leenie like her own breasts more.

"My ma made it for me," she said, sitting up again and lowering the baby onto her lap.

"She didn't want you growed up, huh?"

"It was me didn't want 'em, not so big."

"Well, it ain't your choice, dear, but no matter, you'll learn to like 'em yet." She came around in front of Leenie. The baby had stopped fussing. Hettie talked to her, "Ain't you a good little girl. Yes. Yes you are." She knelt down onto one knee, then very slowly set the other knee down. She smelled powerfully of garlic, garlic and some spice Leenie couldn't guess.

"Now, what could you be hidin' in here?" she said as she reached over the baby and lifted Leenie's shirt.

Obediently, Leenie sat back and let Hettie's blue wrinkly hands untie the laces, pull apart the canvas, reach into the binder, and lift out her left breast. Red blotches marked it from the eyelets pushing into her skin and there were stripes too, going vertical over the nipple, from the boned corset digging in. But floating there in Hettie's palm, her breast seemed to gather itself for a moment, to lift itself up as the air swirled around it and Leenie had to hold her breath so she wouldn't cry.

"Well, well," Hettie said, "this here bosom is lovely."

Leenie felt the blood rush to her face.

Hettie pulled gently on the nipple. "Does that hurt?" Each pull was harder. "Now? Now? Hurt yet?"

It did hurt, but Leenie kept shaking her head. Whenever their daddy woke them up to milk, he'd throw the covers back and as she and Frances lay there hating the cold, he'd laugh and yell, "Come on girls, time to pull tits."

Hettie pulled a last time and then stuck her finger into the baby's mouth and nestled it up against Leenie's nipple, bright red now and smarting. Gradually, Hettie pulled her finger away and the baby's lips closed around the nipple and started sucking. Leenie caved forward.

"Come now, sit up!" Hettie said in a sudden, hard tone. "Just breathe out long and slow. I got the milk warmin'." She stood up as slowly as she had knelt down.

Leenie stared at the baby sucking her breast. It didn't look like it felt. It looked beautiful. Hettie was talking. "Now, each time, you hold the bottle upside down above your bosom so it seems the milk's comin' from you. You got that?

"Let her suck first on your tit and then let her feed from the bottle, go back and forth, back and forth."

Leenie squeezed her eyes. A knifepoint of pain in her chest was closing everything out, Hettie's voice, even the baby. Something inside was being pulled from her, but the opening was just too small.

6

It was the pain on her face Digger noticed first, her mouth downturned and quivering, her eyes slightly closed. After a few days he could tell, even from the stairway, by how she held her shoulders, or how her hair fell. He'd see her rocking the baby by the stove, the bottle next to her, and wait. Soon strings of hair would drop across her cheek, her shoulders would curl in and forward as she lifted her blouse over the baby's face, and he'd move to the shadows in the parlor and watch.

It wasn't for a week at least, maybe two, until he began to look for her breast. He could see just a coin's worth of skin, sometimes less, between the folds of her shirt and his daughter's mouth. But then his daughter would let go to drink from the bottle and he'd see her nipple, dark red and extended. He could feel how much it hurt her and that eased him. He couldn't say why, it was like liquor, the thought of her pain carried him straight to her, he'd stand behind a door, or curtain, and after it was over, after she'd risen, the baby asleep in the basket, and he could breathe again, he was left worse off than before.

Most nights he tried to go to bed, but even if he kept the lantern lit, he saw things. Addie's hands picking at each other when they were idle, her skin rough, dried out from dirt; the small, unruly hairs on her neck as she poured another pot of boiling water into the washtub for her bath, the steam heavy with balsam or lavender.

He crept out of his room then and sat on the top step where up against the wall, half-asleep, he could hear Leenie cry. If he was lucky, he cried too. But as soon as he went back to his bed, the airlessness of his grief closed in again and he repeated over and over the psalm, *All the night make I my bed to swim; I water my couch with my tears,* picturing in the room across the hall Leenie crying or squeezing her eyes shut, her dirty hair on the pillow, her reddened nipples as she lay there with his daughter, still unnamed. It burned, her namelessness, and his helplessness.

One night, when the burning became unbearable, he made his way to the river, soundlessly and without a lantern, though there wasn't much of a moon. The ground was already frozen a few inches down. He went to his spot on the shore, took off his clothes, and rushed in. Four strides and he dove under. The sudden force of the cold pushed in on his chest and stopped his breath. He thrashed about till he could breathe again, in fits and starts, and use the trick he learned as a boy—to find something in the sky, something he could track. He rolled over and found a spot on the moon and stared at it till he could move his limbs calmly, stroking sometimes against, sometimes with the current. He drifted toward the gravel shallows and grabbed a handful of silt for his armpits and another to wash around his anus. He still had some blood on him, mostly under his nails, from the pig he and Burdett had killed. He felt like a boy again, though he knew it wouldn't last. The only thing shutting out the grief was the cold.

He had grown up bathing in the river, in this exact spot. (Every Sunday until the ice began to flow, his mother would check to see if he was clean.) Cold as it was, he didn't want to get out now, knowing what he would feel as he approached the shore, more and more of his body exposed—the magnificence of his skin, tingling and alive. It had been utterly joyful when he was young, like birds in the morning, noisy, fluttering, and even then he sensed it was a church of its own—the river, his body rising into the air. But now, as he came out of the water, his skin felt like glass being shattered. He wasn't prepared for it, or for what overtook him. He had wrapped her body before he lowered her into the hole and then, it took him a long time, but finally and carefully enough he thought, he pulled the sheet across and covered her face. But as he dropped the first shovelful onto her, the sheet slipped back and the dirt hit her neck, the skin over her voice box. He lowered himself in to fix it, but more dirt dropped in with him, kept dropping in, it was hitting her cheek, her hair . . .

Quickly, he rubbed himself off with his shirt, put on his pants, and carrying his long underwear and boots ran into the house. He hung his shirt on the drying rack above the stove, took off his pants and hung them too. He wasn't chilled, though he hovered over the fire so his skin could dry before he put on his union suit and socks.

"Bathing weakens you," his mother always said, making sure he didn't sneak into the river to wash more than once a week, and he knew now how true it was. He made his way upstairs and entered her room.

She lay on the far side facing him, the baby asleep and nestled into her. He spoke softly, "Leenie?"

She cocked her head up from the pillow but didn't speak.

"Leenie? Please." He waited. "Please." He could hear her breaths, deliberate, measured.

"Yes," she finally said and he lifted the blanket and carefully lay his body down around the baby. "But don't touch me."

He didn't need to touch her, he only needed to hear her breathe, and hear his daughter too, between them, her breaths quick and soft. But it was Leenie's breaths, as they became louder and slower, that carried him. With their momentary lift and heavy descent, they carried him down through the dark into sleep.

He woke when his daughter whimpered. There was a shuffling, a cry, then silence. He heard Leenie swallowing, a long breath, more swallowing. Her attention drawn so deeply inward seized him and he clutched onto the psalm: *All the night make I my bed to swim . . .*

He woke again just before daybreak and slipped out.

It became his ritual, the river and her bed, the rhythms of her breathing.

"It ain't fair," Leenie said to him one morning after she set down a plate of sausage, "going through life without a name." She paced back and forth with the baby, tracking a course between the stove and table, from the shed door to the parlor, burping her, then draping the baby over her shoulder and holding her by the feet to bounce the colic out of her belly—what her ma made the girls do with Janey, taking turns during holiday suppers.

Digger started eating. He loved sausage and she had thrown some potatoes in the pan, a few onions.

"Well, you her father?" Leenie said. "Or you gonna just set there and eat?" She held the baby up in front of her. "Don't you worry, I'll get you a name today if I have to buy it. Abigail," Leenie said.

"No," he answered, staring at a jar Leenie had set on the table, the last of the yellow beech leaves with some blades of timothy. And by the sink a twig of balsam in a little milk pitcher, with some winterberry she'd cut. It was strange how girls couldn't leave well enough alone outdoors, felt compelled to drag in this and that. He'd seen it in his ma and grandma too, and in Addie—all through summer, bringing in what was blooming, forget-me-nots, meadow rues, daisies, black-eyed Susans, chicory, Joe-Pye. But why anyone would drag in old grass! Cat's tail, his mother called it, for the seed heads, long past now and about to shed all over.

Leenie shifted the baby to her left side and sat down with her plate. "Betty."

"No."

"Clara."

"No."

"Da . . . Daisy."

"No."

"Elizabeth."

"No! Stop." He'd lived so many years alone, it came as a surprise when he married. Not just the flowers. He'd watch the bedcovers thrown back each morning, the sweep of Addie's arm across the bottom sheet, the covers tucked and pulled tight, and though he liked the house kept clean, he wondered about the usefulness of such tidiness, such domesticity—the curtains and rugs and upholstery just so.

Leenie heaped a spoonful of Addie's rhubarb jelly on her potatoes.

"On potatoes?"

"Francesca."

"Stop."

"Gertrude."

"Stop. No." First married, he didn't understand, but he saw them now, the little bouquets and such, for what they were— weapons. On a table here, by a sink there, they each did their part, keeping the darkness at bay. Even the sausage browned and served hot. The kitchen felt it, the table felt it, pine boards his grandpa had nailed together as a young man, marked and oiled with years of linseed, and lighter now. Though a jar of spent timothy, that beat all.

"Harriet."

"No." He pushed his empty plate away, put on his coat. He wasn't going to waste any more time with this naming nonsense.

It was a clear day and he could smell the cold—fresh and sharp—a few whiffs of sourness coming from the orchard, some apples rotting. And smoke too, drifting through the slats of the smokehouse. The ground was hard, sealed tight, they hadn't had a real snow yet, just a few coverings that melted off by noon or midmorning. When he woke, there'd been an inch or so on each of the locust posts—small white puffs against the dark like so many hats in a line, but they were gone now. He carried a few armloads of wood into the smokehouse, checked the fire, the shoulders and hams hanging from the joists. Then he followed the sound of the ax through the lower field, past a trickle of hay where Burdett had carried out a few sheaves for the horses. A dusting of snow still lay in the shadows. November seemed kind to him. The oaks were bare and he could see through the woods to the ledges on the ridge and the contours of Mount Pisgah, Balsam, and in back of that, Mary Smith, mostly white now.

Burdett was already down on the bank behind the field where the dump was. Ash trees had shot up on the slope like weeds and Digger had been wanting to cut them ever since they started to lean. He thought of it every time he threw junk over the bank. But last week a storm blew down half of the oldest, tallest ash and the next day Burdett didn't disappear home like he usually did after he was finished, he stalled. "Mr. Benton?" Digger closed the gate after the chickens and looked over at him. "We could cut those ashes you been talkin' about," and Digger nodded and said, "Sunday."

When Burdett saw Digger approach, he put down his ax, he'd already gotten a chestnut out of the way, been dead a few years now. It had dried standing and Burdett was chopping it up for firewood. The two-man saw was leaning against one of the larger ashes and Digger picked it up, checking which would be the next tree, the path of its fall, the angle of the cut. Most of them were the right size—two, two and a half feet thick. He hadn't ever liked ashes—they didn't leaf out sometimes till the middle of June and the boles shot up so straight and regular they looked unnatural, though they did bring in money (more even than the cherry after they got defoliated by the army worms and were ruined forever for veneer). Roger Lyman would give him nearly $30 a load to truck the ash to Sherwood's mill for baseball bats and broom handles.

Burdett walked downhill of the tree Digger was studying and took hold of the other end of the saw. They turned it and set the teeth against the bark. They eyed each other as Digger positioned the angle of the saw and slowly started to pull while Burdett gave, and then Burdett pulled while Digger gave and in three or four strokes, one pulling, the other giving, they fell into the long, low rhythm of a sharp saw.

They heard the whistle blasts from the train rolling in from East Branch, and every hour, bells from Reverend Sims's church. Digger liked hearing the whistle but not the bells, they made him nervous. He'd work faster for a while, at the saw or chopping up the branches, and Burdett would change his pace to match. Burdett spoke whenever he had to but he usually didn't find the need so the only two things Digger knew about his life were that he'd never been a churchgoer and that a few years back he walked up Jump Hill one night to find Hettie Brower and bring her back to town to help him with a girl about to give birth. And Digger only found out about that through Jimmy.

It was Jimmy that picked Hettie and Burdett up that night on their way back to town and without asking who the girl was or why it was Burdett who had to fetch Hettie, he drove them to Mr. Kolb's place—the man who owned half the county's acid factories. Burdett took them back behind the barn into the chicken coop and there was Jenny Kolb, the fat girl, not yet eighteen, and terrified. They couldn't move her, the baby was already coming in the middle of all that stink and with the chickens carrying on louder than she did. Jimmy left then, but later Hettie told him Burdett was as good as any woman helping, and maybe better too, because a rooster kept rushing Jenny until Burdett grabbed it from behind and ran out and however he did it no one knows but the next morning they saw the rooster's head was knocked in and there wasn't a sledge in sight. No one ever found out either if it was his baby or he was just being kind. If Hettie knew, she wouldn't tell.

Digger rigged up Dan and Johnny and they skidded four trees out by noon, dragged off a few branches for firewood. Burdett went home, he never ate in the house, even holidays, even when Addie was cooking, and Digger walked into the kitchen, hoping to eat hot food, hoping the baby had slept some.

"What'd you make?" he asked, smelling mostly onions cooking.

"Isabel. Julia. Katherine." He should've guessed she had a stubborn streak. Her face was all lit up like Sam's when he was up to some prank.

He looked into the basket. "How long she been asleep?"

"Lucy."

She loved this game, didn't she. He sat down at his place and called Teddy over, scraped some burrs off him, combing his hands through the hair on the dog's neck and chest while he waited. She hung the dish towel she was using on the drying rack and scooped a ladle of food onto a plate, set it in front of him, steaming.

"Mary."

He handed her a fistful of burrs to throw in the stove. He meant it as an answer and he could tell by her face she took it as one, but she wasn't going to give up.

"Nellie."

He took off his cap and shook out his napkin. The food looked like some sort of stew. He forked through it—onions, potatoes, carrots, leeks, onions, turnips, chard, more onions, some pork, thank God.

"Anything not in here?" he asked.

"Ophelia!" She was at the stove, eating out of the pot, even though her place was set. "Penelope."

He reached for the salt. He was hoping Leenie would've made dough balls soaked with pulled pork, but it was alright, what Addie would've called serviceable—she was fussier than he was.

"Qua . . . Queenie."

He tasted some kale, she even threw in kale. Just like her ma: use everything you got, though Edith *had* to, making do with nothing. He added more salt.

"Rebecca."

Rebecca. That was it. He turned around. "Rebecca."

"Rebecca?"

He nodded. "Rebecca."

She lowered her head toward the basket. "How you like that? Rebecca. Rebecca Benton. Yes, Rebecca fits her. She *is* a Rebecca. Rebecca Benton." Then she turned to him. "Did you know that all along? Did you? Look at me, Uncle Willis, I'm askin' you somethin'." She was glaring at him.

"Digger."

"Digger. Did you know her name all along? Did you? Look at me."

The name *had* come to him one night in the river. Thoughts would rush in with his breath when it came back after the first shock, and he let them go, all of them, while he swayed in the current. But he knew it wasn't that simple.

"Not exactly," he said, meeting her eye for a moment.

"Not exactly? And you never said nothin'! We've gone two weeks like this."

She was right. The name changed things. It was as if the baby wasn't completely born till she was named, she was still with Addie.

During the day, Leenie would say it over and over, *Rebecca, Rebecca girl,* while she was sweeping the kitchen or the steps to the shed, or wringing out clothes or at the sink, washing the smoked-up lamp chimneys, or scrubbing radishes or carrots or parsnips. And at night too. But he couldn't, not out loud. He knew the silence would ride up on the last syllables, the *becca,* and swallow any other words. It was Addie's silence mostly, and where the name came from too, the silence of the river—clear and inhuman.

But listening to her daily singsong of *Rebecca, Rebecca girl,* he began to whisper it to himself under his breath. At first, it would sweep his mind clean, filling every cranny so all of his thoughts were rolled into a single unified feeling, a feeling that was only her name, repeating itself indefinitely. *Rebecca* became so loud in his mind he couldn't tell exactly when it broke out of his mouth, though he knew it was in the barn, his forehead leaning on some cow's ribs, Burdett humming across the aisle, the milk squirting into the pail. That's when he first heard himself, though he couldn't guess how long he'd been saying it.

At night they started to say it, *Rebecca,* back and forth, as she lay between them, saying it to her, over her. He'd put his hand on her little back or belly, her whole belly fit under his palm, and drift off to sleep. When he woke—before Leenie, before dawn—he'd leave as quietly as he could. Once when he woke late, the sky already pale, he glanced back from the door at the bed. Leenie had wrapped herself around the baby, and the covers had slipped down off her shoulder. He walked back— she was too skinny for the cold. For a moment he paused, fixed above her, his arms slightly raised. There was a thin ribbon sewn around the neck of her nightgown—it was worn and washed of color, though it might have been lavender once or blue. Then he pulled the blankets over her and left.

He knew the exact moment the milk came. He was in his spot behind the drapes in the parlor. Leenie was in her spot too, their spot, in the rocker by the cookstove. She made an odd sound, held Rebecca away and lifted her right breast, twisting it close to her face. The nipple was swollen and shiny. Just before she dropped her breast and brought the baby close again, a drip fell. Rebecca latched on and Leenie's head rolled back, she rocked in circles, making singsongy sounds, cooing sounds, sounds of relief, of joy, and he felt it too. His whole body was flooded with joy, a joy he hadn't felt since Addie, and he started rocking with her, until he noticed the curtains were moving. He stopped, realizing he was a man hiding, watching a girl, his niece, nurse a baby.

That evening, after Rebecca was asleep, Digger was by the stove fixing and cleaning a harness when Leenie tromped through the kitchen with a towel and a bar of her mother's lye soap. Straps of leather hung everywhere, from the hooks holding the frying pans, over the backs of chairs, on the stool, lined up on the table.

"Where *you* goin'?"

She stopped just outside the circle of light. He could barely see her, still facing the door.

"The river."

"You gonna take your clothes off?"

She turned toward him. "I'm gonna bathe."

"It's too cold for you."

"I ain't some city girl."

"Getting more fond of that word *ain't*, aren't ya?"

"Around you I am."

"Don't go out there."

"What are you sayin', Uncle Willis? I gotta bathe too."

"Digger."

"Digger."

"That's better." He put the awl down on the stool beside him and turned up the flame. She backed farther into the dark.

"You're gonna be naked in there," he said.

"I'm gonna bathe!"

"You're gonna take it from me." He stood up, the room darkened. "You're gonna take the river from me." He went toward her and she backed against the door. He could smell the soap, the plain lye, her ma boiling the ashes and never adding a hint of herb or perfume. He grabbed her forearms. She didn't try to twist out of his hold, she lowered her head—like a horse ready to buck; he knew it but he didn't let go.

"I seen you watchin'." The words were aimed at the floor, but then she looked up at him and said very slowly, "I have seen you, Uncle Willis, watchin'."

He let go of her, turned away, and the door slammed.

7

Leenie followed his tracks, the path Uncle Willis took each night through the hardhack down to a small stretch of dirt by the river. On each side of the opening, the bank fell steeply, carved out by high water and grown up again with Joe-Pye and willow. In the low light, she could see a rock large enough to put her things on, the towel and clean underclothes wrapped inside. She took off everything except her underpants. She was going home tomorrow for Thanksgiving supper and she was determined to go home clean.

She put her hands in the water first, waited till her wrists turned numb. Her skin wasn't burning—he didn't grip her hard like her daddy did, with her daddy she would try to twist free—but she still needed the cold even more than she needed to bathe. Cold was too much feeling and the end of feeling all in one, it was feeling burst into nothingness.

She took off her underpants, lifted out the rag inside them. Both of them were soaked with blood. She stepped into the river and submerged them—there was still enough light to see the dark rough cloud spread under the water, which was dark too, but shinier. *Dark inside dark.* The words repeated like a chorus. She shook the rag till all the new blood washed away and there was no difference in the darks. Then she washed them with her mama's soap and wrung them out.

She had never bathed in so much water. The little stream she and Frances washed in each week downhill from the barn was so low every August, they had to dig out a hollow to catch enough water to sit down in. But this . . . this was immersion, or could be. Not tonight. She wouldn't go under tonight. She ran in up to her thighs, squatted, then stood in one quick motion. She was shivering hard. She squatted again just long enough to wash away the soap. The lye had already started to burn. Then quickly she toweled dry and with her hands shaking, folded the clean rag into her underpants, pulled on her union suit, and ran back to the house.

Uncle Willis was still in the rocker by the stove fixing the harness, Rebecca beside him in the basket, asleep. Long strips of leather fitted with buckles and rings hung everywhere around, the hames draped over the broom hook. She didn't care he was there, she was too cold to care, she dropped her clothes and shoes by the door, threw her wet things on the rack, and hovered over the stove. He didn't raise his head or say a word. After a while, her shivering slowed down. She swallowed back tears, but they kept coming, circling up from her throat through the back of her head into her eyes.

She hadn't cried since those long nights before the milk came, not even on the walks she took now so she wouldn't feel cooped up. Not even the day she found the new church down the road with all the people pouring out into the yard—town, valley, and hill people too, talking and laughing while the reverend stood at the door and shook everyone's hand, here and there pinching a baby's cheek or making a woman smile and patting his big belly or looking into a farmer's eyes and nodding as if he were a farmer himself—even seeing that from behind the hydrangeas didn't make her cry. Or the red quilt either, hanging out in the sun—the sole bit of color in the valley, everything having turned to brown or gray over the past month, and the sky too, seeming to favor gray. Even that red didn't make her cry, though she felt the want keenly enough, not only for that quilt but for a bed to lay it upon, a normal bed in a normal household where a normal man and a normal woman could talk about more than just who was going to take the baby so the other could eat, they'd talk about things they loved and dreamed about and longed for.

Now the tears wouldn't stop. It was the kind of crying her daddy called "thawing out" and it was true, she *was* thawing, something was breaking up, breaking free inside, and it was more than just cold.

Uncle Willis set the awl down on the footstool. She heard the bulk of leather and hardware drop to the floor, the empty rocker rocking beside her. He came from behind, his smell and then his arms closing around her. At first she tightened, squeezed her eyes shut, but he was so warm he was like a second stove, her shoulders and back gave way until she was leaning into him, he was holding her up. "It's alright, it's alright," he repeated each time her shivering started again. After a while the cold disappeared, and as it did, the line between her body and his disappeared too. That frightened her and she stopped leaning against him and stood on her own. He backed away, sat down, and picked up the awl.

He didn't go out to the river that night or come into her room. He stayed on the top step like he used to do, and he was still there the next morning in his boots and day clothes, his head cocked against the wall, his dark hair messed and curled over his collar. Teddy lay right beside him. There was a bottle of whiskey on the second step down and he had the smell on him, the smell she'd grown up with. She didn't wake him. She put pillows on either side of Rebecca and snuck downstairs to load the stove. Today, she was going home and bringing with her a smoked ham.

She couldn't remember spending a Thanksgiving at home. Every year her family had piled into the Model T, Osmer's Revenge, or before that the wagon, to come here, the house of plenty. Uncle Willis must've pondered on that too, because he'd gone to Lloyd's and arranged for Old Man Richard to deliver Mama coffee, sugar, salt, pepper, cloves, cinnamon, allspice, even flour—she always ran out of her own—so she could cook up a storm for the holiday, and he had Leenie write out her sisters' favorite things. Saltwater taffy for Frances. Peppermint candies for Mary. Peanut brittle for Janey. She added chocolates for Mama, which Emma could suck on too. And root beer for everybody. When he read the list, he asked Leenie what she wanted. She stalled, hoping she wouldn't have to say it out loud, but she did finally, as low as she could, "Licorice," knowing his mouth would straighten into a thin line before he turned away because after a holiday meal, Addie would bring out licorice. It was her favorite thing too, and everybody would watch as Leenie and Addie bit down on each end of the stick and ate toward each other. Then they'd both start laughing and Addie would let go and Leenie'd eat the rest of it.

Leenie was measuring out coffee grounds when Digger came downstairs carrying the baby against his chest, his large hand covering her back.

"You're up early," he said. His left cheek had a red blotch where it had been pushed against the wall. "Barely light."

She nodded. "It's Thanksgivin'."

He leaned over the basket and started to lower Rebecca in.

"Don't, not yet. She'll wake."

But he dropped onto his knee and laid the baby down anyway. "There," he whispered as he slid his arms very slowly out from under her, "there."

Leenie stopped moving as she watched Rebecca's face turn to the left and squinch. Her mouth opened and puckered once, twice—and then, as if sleep were a wand waved over her, her face softened and went still and Leenie let out a long, thankful breath. Nothing as angelic as the face of a sleeping child, her grandma used to say, a mother of thirteen, and even the young ones caught the bitterness in her tone.

Digger bunched up his shirtsleeves, leaned against the sink, and splashed water on his face. "Thanksgivin'," he said and groaned as he turned his head to the side. "I'm just askin' to get through the day."

"Askin' who?" Leenie said as she took the sugar bowl from the shelf.

He stayed hunched over his forearms, his brown wool shirt stretched across his shoulders and back. The long muscle running down the right of his spine was larger than the one on the left, from the one-sided work he'd done since he was a boy— pitching hay, shoveling manure.

"Just askin'," he finally said, his face still pointed toward the drain as he grabbed the hand towel. He was a large and foreign country.

"You're not askin' the Lord?"

He didn't answer, but she knew. He had stopped mentioning the Lord. Even the psalm he recited so much lately didn't mention the Lord, it was about night and bed and tears.

He started sweeping as he'd taken to doing every morning, and the sound soothed her, the rhythm changing just enough to keep her listening. Rebecca started to fuss, but Leenie didn't rush to her. She got the cream from the back wall of the shed and poured their coffee—now that she had let down milk, she could wait, Rebecca was easy to quiet. Hettie had been right.

Leenie didn't give enough milk to keep the baby fed but at least it held her for a while—she didn't whimper while Louise's milk was warming. Finally Leenie lifted Rebecca out of the basket and sat down. Digger set the broom aside, and as soon as she raised her shirt to start nursing, he leaned against the sink and looked straight at her.

So he wasn't going to stop watching.

Her face flushed and she felt almost dizzy, but she didn't get up and move, she pulled apart her makeshift binder and right along with him, looked down as Rebecca's mouth bobbed in the air and took hold of her nipple. Then, out of the blue like a gift, a small but saving grace, came a song from her childhood and she started to sing.

Mama kill me
Daddy eat me
Sister crack my marrow bones
Bury me under cold dark stones
Cold dark stones . . .

Digger broke out laughing. "That is one gruesome song."

"It is? My grandma always sung it to us—to sleep."

"To sleep? Nah!"

"Sung it to all of us, but it was always Mary's favorite. It's about a child turned into a little bird. That's just the chorus— what I remember. I've always loved the tune. I guess I never thought about how gruesome the words are, but they are, aren't they?"

"You're a wonder, you."

"Me? Why?"

"Yes, you. And I sure ain't gonna tell you why." He smiled that same smile that had surprised her so on her first morning there.

She watched him out the sink window, though she knew his route by now—chicken coop smokehouse barn, or smokehouse chicken coop barn, in through the big door, out the milk-house door. Her ma would've frowned, she never walked out a different door than the one she came in through. It would bring on Trouble—a hurt animal, sickness, or even once, another child. She and her sisters never minded the doors, what they hated were the black cats. They'd take the morning to fix a picnic and they'd be almost to where they were going when a black cat would cross the road and Mama would turn right around and go home. No ifs, ands, or buts. Sometimes Leenie and Frances would swear up and down the Bible (which her ma never read but still would swear upon) that they saw white on the cat's face or chest, any place they didn't think she saw. Most of the time, they'd turn around anyway and Frances would pout for a week and complain that right down the road were children being raised by *modern* parents. But even Frances would touch down on a chair if she forgot something and had to go back into the house. They all did that, that's why they left a stool right inside the door.

She bundled up Rebecca and tucked her in the baby carriage. She had a couple of hours before they had to leave so she could take their usual walk—away from town, past the Schultz farm— where all the buildings and fences got painted white every couple years because, as everyone explained, the Schultzes were from Germany—and then up a side road that circled behind the creamery where the trucks backed in to dump off their milk, along with a few wagons, enough for her to watch out she didn't roll the carriage through a pile of manure. Some of the men nodded or tipped their hats as she walked by, a few younger ones she recognized from school, though they were older than she was by a few years—Randy Butler, Clayton Buell, Will Miller—just now taking on their fathers' farms, doing their fathers' bidding.

The road came out by Emmett's Inn, where her daddy told her he'd often go to hear Emmett play fiddle after supper, which she figured was at least partly true. And then the place her mama called the house of ill repute, lowering her voice as she mentioned to her two oldest girls rumors of the lost angels, the children who never got born. The house was unpainted, an overgrown tangle of shrub roses (still with a few hips) crowding in on the front door, all the curtains pulled shut. Leenie hoped she'd see the lady, Pretty Margaret. Just from the sound of her name Leenie imagined her wearing an evening gown—dark velvet, blue or maybe a deep green—coming in tight around her waist and then swirling north and south around her hips and bosoms, her shoulders very white and her thin arms spread wide. But Leenie didn't see anyone. There was no sign of life at all, not even any manure, though her uncles on more than one holiday had joked about the few piles often left there in front. "Only three men in town would still hitch up a wagon to go to that woman," one of them would start and another would chime back, "and two of 'em are 'bout dead," and they'd laugh and spit, thinking about the story that led to that manure.

A few doors down was the old Presbyterian church that long ago was sold to the Catholics and covered now with Virginia creeper, a few of its red leaves still hanging on. Then the new church, which two Sundays running Leenie snuck up on to watch the people pouring forth. But now, almost nine o'clock Thanksgiving morning, there wasn't a car in sight. She started to walk by. Until she heard singing—a piano too, though that wasn't what stopped her. It was the singing, a man's singing—an old hymn she didn't know, but it didn't matter, the words didn't matter. She lifted Rebecca from the carriage and carried her along the east side of the church beneath the high windows till she found one propped open just a few inches, and there, above her head, the man's voice called out to the Lord, almost desperately pleading for the Lord who was far far away, and Leenie, holding Rebecca, swayed and cried—the very same crying she'd done the night before until he—her uncle—came from behind and wrapped himself around her.

By the time Leenie got back, Digger had already turned his truck around and pointed it toward the road. It was a Larrabee, a ton truck he bought straight from the company in Binghamton, painted green and only two years old—not like Osmer's Revenge at all, it had a starter on the inside you didn't have to crank, and a door on the driver's side and door handles too, that you could open from the outside.

Leenie handed Rebecca to her uncle and hurried about—it was past ten and she hadn't yet gathered what she was bringing home, a jar of Addie's pickles they always had with Mama's pot cheese and Frances's gloves, the ones Frances got for her birthday and made Leenie take. "To remember me by!" Frances had said and Leenie had rolled her eyes (and immediately wished she hadn't). But now Frances needed them more than Leenie did, Addie had gloves Uncle Willis would let her wear. Then for Mary, another Christina Rossetti book from Addie's bookshelf.

Some rhubarb jam for Janey. A ribbon for Emma. She ran out. He had already started the motor. She set the basket on the floor of the truck, climbed in, and took Rebecca back. Uncle Willis looked awful—his face somber and worn as an old tree.

He'd been to her home only once before—when Wade died and her daddy was gone. Addie stayed with Mama indoors while Uncle Willis milked the cows and cleaned the gutters, then found some wood, a few nails, and a saw and built Wade a little box and Mama always loved him for that. "You children joke about Willis's queer rantin's," she'd say, "but he helped me when I needed it most." Then, in a lower tone, she'd add, "Deep down, he's a kindly man."

They took the River Road toward town. When they got closer to the church, Leenie blurted out, "That's where the man was singin'," though she stopped short of mentioning she'd hidden in the bushes to watch the people pouring forth.

Digger kept his eyes on the road as they passed where she was pointing. "What man?"

"There was a man singin' inside—with just a gorgeous voice." She pulled the lap robe over her legs and tucked it behind Rebecca's head.

They crossed Main Street on the corner where Lloyd's store was, the post office in the room off the back. On the opposite side was Sal's Place (a barbershop and spaghetti house both together).

"That's Sims," he finally said. "You stay clear of him, you hear?"

She'd heard *that* name plenty—the man Aunt Addie used to call a rat "no matter he's a minister" and the man Uncle Willis railed against the night he burned her casket.

"Why?" she asked.

He didn't answer, but after they passed out of town through the covered bridge he started to pontificate, although the motor was so loud as they headed up Mary Smith Hill, she could barely hear him.

"The World is not just as you see it . . . made not of matter only . . . the World has a soul . . . a soul the Lord has done His best to steal . . ."

Did he say *steal?*

". . . steal and call His Own in order that men might see it. Blind men, Leenie. Take these fields, Lloydrick Butler's fields . . ."

They didn't look like much, the ground black and frozen where in the summer stood rows of cauliflower, but she was getting used to his voice rising and falling as if he were talking to a congregation.

"And see . . . the soil beneath and the sweat poured into that soil . . . and hear if you can the steady pace of the oxen, the mark of their . . . the scrape of the iron plow upon the rocks . . . And think on the . . . who forged the plow, Leenie, is not his skill also lodged there? And what of they who made the forge and . . . a line of men that goes back and back, and women too, and horses and machines . . . the felled trees . . . no other field . . . as this one. Amen."

She couldn't help but smile at the thought of the Lord sneaking around stealing.

"You callin' the Lord a criminal?" she said.

"Oh, Leenie, understand—only that blind men might see."

"He *has* to steal, then?"

"Yes." He nodded. "So that men might see a World behind the world we see before us."

"See two worlds, then?"

"What?"

"Two worlds?"

He nodded and shifted into third as they got to the flats.

"But the Lord doesn't have to steal on *your* account?"

"My eyes have been torn open," he said.

She spotted a self-satisfied sheen on his face. "So you're allowed to call the Lord a criminal?"

"I didn't use that word."

"You said He steals."

"The World is endowed with a soul, its own soul, but the Lord has called it His."

"So He stole it."

"Yes."

"You're as strange as they say you are."

She looked down at his hand, full of veins and dark from the sun, and as if she were testing paraffin on a new jar of jelly, she touched it.

He started. "What?"

She didn't answer, and he went on talking. Leenie held the baby's head steady. This road pocked with holes and ruts was her road now.

Frances heard the truck even before the dog did and was all the way down to where the road split off to the barn, with Janey right behind her, sucking her fingers.

"Stop, I'll get out here before you park," Leenie said, feeling the old knot in her stomach. She knew by how Frances was holding herself by the elbows and how Janey was clinging to Frances's skirt. After dreaming of them laughing around the table, singing together, here was the truth again, colliding on in: it was Thanksgiving, another holiday, and Mama had turned mean.

And neither of 'em with coats, Leenie said to herself as she stepped off the running board. The truck pulled toward the flat spot by the barn and they ran toward her, Frances's face blotchy with tears. Leenie tightened her hold on Rebecca.

As Leenie hugged them, Frances and Janey cried, but finally, they spit the story out. For a few months, Mama had been wondering where all her chicks were going, she thought maybe it was Charlie Owen's dog.

"It was Janey!" Frances said. "When the grass died back on the bank, Mama saw—"

"She saw the bones!" Janey said.

"Janey would pick the little chicks up like we all used to do, and she'd hold 'em and squeeze 'em till I'd look over and see their guts was popped out. She didn't mean nothin', did ya, Janey? We've all killed a few chicks.

"Oh, she can just *ruin* the most specialest of days!" Frances sniffled. "And then I gotta stand there and she makes Janey stand there too, and watch while she draws her hand back clear to the wall, I swear, I almost hit her back, I could, I'm big enough. She's been a whole lot worse since you been gone, Leenie," Frances said. "She's just a bitch!"

"I know, I know." Leenie stroked Frances's hair back away from her wet cheeks. "She just *is,* and there's nothin' we can do about it."

And then Janey whispered so softly they could barely hear it, "Bitch," and it sounded so fresh, so beautiful coming from her lips that Leenie and Frances started to laugh and Janey was all pleased and proud and Frances wiped Janey's face with the blanket hanging down from the baby.

"So this is Addie's girl?" Frances asked.

"Little Rebecca," Leenie answered and held the baby away from her shoulder so they could look at her. Janey touched her cheek very softly.

"She's a pretty little thing," Frances said and brought her face in close, "Ain't ya? Ain't ya?" Then she looked up to Leenie again. "It was all goin' so well, she was in a pretty good mood, and I made sweet potatoes just covered in syrup and Mary made an apple pie with the top in the shape of an *L* and you better notice, even though it's impossible to make out the *L,* you better make a big scene or she'll be crushed, she worked so hard and it just got worse, and Ma's there sayin', Never handle the crust more'n you have to, Mary, and she's at the table just mauling it, tears runnin' down her face. So don't you forget and you better not laugh neither."

"Either."

"Either."

By the time they reached the house, the ham was sitting on the Hoosier looking twice as big in the crowded kitchen.

"Willis's outside doin' *your* chores," Mama said and turned to Leenie. "Hi, dear." She threw her hand toward Frances, whisking her away with it. "I know you two been talkin' but you don't know the half of it, Leenie, what I been through." She threw her hand again. "With these children!"

Leenie gave her mama a kiss but threw Frances a look that said they were still on the same side.

Leenie and Mary walked out to the horse barn. The scrapes on Lady's sides were almost healed. Mary grabbed a milk stool to stand on and started combing burrs out of the mare's mane. Leenie used her fingers. Outside of their ma's territory, they could talk however they wanted. Leenie told Mary what she thought in the truck, how words sometimes hide and you can't find them.

"I think words live in families. Like we do," Mary answered right back.

Leenie was untangling part of Lady's mane. "You think some words work too hard and get worn out?"

"Like Ma's pet word *appreciate*. If I hear that again," Mary said. Lady raised her head then, and Mary ended up with a wad of horsehair in the comb. She threw the hair on the floor.

"We don't have to save this?" Leenie asked.

Mary shook her head. "Take forever to clean out the burrs. We throw it in the burn barrel now, we just don't tell her."

Leenie brushed a few prickers from her fingers. "Some words love each other," she said.

"Do they walk together and hold hands?" Mary whispered, smiling.

"And kiss," Leenie added, giggling as if she were in grade school. They made up a game then, Leenie called out a word and Mary called back its mate.

"Bread."

"Pudding."

"Christmas."

"Morning."

"Hunger."

"Pang."

"Slow."

"Up."

"Slow."

"Down. Slow's a two-timer!" Mary called out and Leenie laughed, wondering where Mary learned that word.

"All done, girl," Mary said, scratching the mare's withers.

Leenie stood back from the wads of horsehair on the floor and lifted up Lady's tail. "So she hasn't come into heat again?"

Mary shook her head as she rubbed Lady's face, the broad flat part between her eyes. "And Mama just won't let up about it."

They'd never had such a supper as that Thanksgiving meal. There were mashed potatoes and turnips, buttered parsnips, buttered carrots, buttered beets, butternut squash, acorn squash, Frances's sweet potatoes, applesauce "with boughten cinnamon," Mama pointed out for Uncle Willis's benefit. They had pot cheese and Polish pot cheese loaded with chopped onions and pepper. There were Addie's pickles and pickled cabbage and pickled cauliflower and watermelon rinds, and some kale nobody touched. There was so much food it had to be rotated on and off the table, and every time the ham came around, Mary said, "Thank you, pig, for being killed so we can eat you."

"Now, there's a grace," Uncle Willis said. He had shaken his head when Mama asked him to say grace, as if they were back at his and Addie's going by their rules—in this home they never said grace. And Mama put Uncle Willis at the head of the table where their daddy used to sit. Uncle Willis didn't say anything more, though, and Leenie realized her sisters had never seen him when he wasn't pontificating.

Mary carried out her apple pie and Leenie made a big fuss, but then Frances mouthed to Mama, "Never handle the crust . . ." and they started to giggle and couldn't stop, her ma pushing her hand in under her breast to hold in her hernia.

Leenie whispered in Mary's ear, "It's you I miss most."

"I don't have anyone to talk to anymore," Mary said, a tear sliding down her cheek, which Leenie kissed, "not about things, *our* things."

"I don't either," Leenie whispered back. "No one smart like you." She thought of the burnt piece of satin in her trunk, how Mary would've turned it into a princess's dress and then into the princess herself, captured in a miniature castle.

Mary stared at Mama and Frances. "Look at 'em, laughin' at me."

"Oh, come on, Mary, honey," Frances said, "I didn't mean nothing, Mama and I were just havin' a good time."

"At my expense," she answered.

"Where do you learn to talk like that?" Mama said. Leenie squeezed Mary's arm. Two peas in a pod, their daddy always called them.

After the pie, Mama brought out the candies she'd hidden. "A present from Uncle Willis. You all say thank you now." Janey yelled thank you the loudest and then they all started "yummin'," as they called it. As they were eating their candy, Uncle Willis said, "I hear, Edith, you got a pregnant mare out there."

"Ask *Leenie* about that," Mama said.

Rebecca squalled, and Leenie got up to nurse. Frances dragged the rocker out from the corner, closer to the stove.

Mama was saying, "I ain't been able to put a harness over those wounds, but she still eats, don't she?"

Frances dipped her head toward Leenie's breast. "What's it like?"

"Ain't bad," Leenie said. "Now that it doesn't hurt."

"Did it hurt bad?"

Leenie shrugged. She was keeping an ear open toward the dinner table.

"I know now, Leenie, it ain't easy bein' the oldest."

Leenie stopped herself from rolling her eyes. Only a month in and Frances knew what being oldest was all about. She couldn't help taking even *that* for her own. Leenie held out her hand. Frances had tears in her eyes.

After Rebecca fell asleep, Leenie whispered, "I think it's safe now to get up," and they both went back to the table. Mama saw them coming and fell silent, though her mouth stayed tight.

Uncle Willis turned to Leenie and opened his arms for the baby.

"Asleep," Leenie said as she handed her over to him, "she doesn't need a bottle." Then she mouthed, "Let's go."

He nodded and stood and as she backed away, she saw her mama staring at them.

While Leenie kissed all her sisters good-bye, Uncle Willis waited outside. Mama stayed by the door. "That's Addie's red coat, ain't it?" It was the first time anyone said Addie's name all night.

"Her old garden coat," Leenie said.

Mama grabbed her arm. "You get pregnant, Leenie, and you ain't ever, ever comin' near this house again, you hear me? Not unless you're married. And don't you kid yourself, your father said the same, you won't walk through this door."

PART II

The farmer who farms land that comes up through his family, he doesn't walk over his property and see it like you or I would, gliding over the top. He's planted hip-deep into the soil himself, or I should say buried, so when the corn or sorghum or buckwheat rises out of the ground toward the sky, he rises too, it's his chance to rise, and that makes him feel every drop of rain and every bit of sun helping him do so, not to mention the droughts and winds and floods standing in his way, and when each crop gets cut down, he too shrinks back toward the soil. And after all that rising and all that shrinking and the weather in between, winter arrives as a welcome rest. The ground grows hard and seals itself up and the farmer inside the farmer can sleep. Not all of him, of course—cold doesn't stop his give-and-take with the animals—but a lot of him.

It's the farm that owns him, not the other way around, which is right since it's the farm that birthed him. And all that the words his land *or* his farm *hold—the ground, the tilth of the soil, the track of the sun, the trees, the water running through it, the fields for crops, the pastures where animals turn grass into flesh or milk—all that isn't something he likes or doesn't like—in fact, most days he's either cussing about it or swearing upon it, because it's kin and there's no divorcing kin, as long as he's him, he's stuck.*

I'm talking, of course, about Digger.

8

Around quarter to one on a dark day in December, Digger drove his truck into the lot at the back of Fletcher Hall. Les Fenton was already there and Woodrow Larkin and Ed Whittaker and George Hull though he hurt his hip, and his son David, and Claude and Letha Kelly. Fuzzy Stone and his son Wayne had walked over from their farm, and of course Jake was there, shaking his head. "I told you so—they're talkin' about the whole valley." And Don Elwood and Don Gordon and his wife, Ina, and Ward Smith and Al Reinhart and Pop Schultz and Sal Placieri, the Italian, and all the Lloyds and Inez Altman, the postmistress, and just as it began to rain and everyone headed inside, Josephine pulled up in her Tin Lizzie, ready to fight, she said, to the last farm. Or you watch, she raised her fist, the City'll take even our graves.

After they'd set out what they thought were enough chairs, Reverend Sims walked in wearing a fur hat and a black wool coat that only partially hid his belly. Seeking out those within his fold, he took both their hands in his and nodded. Yes, he knew his brother's pain, his new church and the even newer back hall he just got built being threatened as well.

The townsfolk kept pouring in, sixty-eight chairs already filled, and about twenty more men standing against the walls.

Even Peg Bridges, who some called Pretty Margaret, managed to make it, turning a few heads, but Inez found a seat for her just the same, right in the middle of the Catholics. As the men moved their knees to the side to make room for Peg to pass— tall, shameless, her dark hair falling from its loose bun in small sprays around her face—each one looked like he could have used a quick sign of the cross. Digger could see from her coat the rain had turned to a light snow.

Once the doors were shut, Inez stood up and said in her booming voice that if everyone could hush, she'd do her best to separate truth from rumor. The room quieted almost instantly. This past Monday, she began, three men—surveyors—came into the post office. Of course they didn't admit to anything, said it was just a geographic survey, and that caused some grumbling and nay-saying in the room. But, she went on, they had *water* written all over them, and *New York City* too, and she sent her son, Ernie, to follow them, and wouldn't you know they followed the exact contour that would lay out a new Route 30, clear as day. Then Harry Samuelson, who owned the garage, stood up. On that same Monday, he had filled the cars of these three men with gas and overheard where they were headed, and he concurred fully with Ernie's report.

Then one at a time men stood to state and restate their grievances against the City, its greed, its insatiable thirst. Wouldn't you think with the dams at Croton, Roundout, and now Ashokan, they'd have enough? Why even with the new tunnel running water from Gilboa, City eyes still roamed over the valley.

None of the Germans or Italians or Irish stood to talk but most of them nodded and yayed with the others. A few of those gathered shook their heads and swore it wasn't going to happen. Not in their lifetime. Others kept shouting *Shinhopple* until Charlie Kidd from the shoe-repair shop stood up. The dam, he said, might not be built north of Downsville at all but thirty miles south in Shinhopple. A boring operation had been done there three years ago. But then Les Fenton said a Water Board employee had stated that boring in no way indicated where a dam would be located. Almost everyone had some different scrap of information and an opinion.

"Condemnation of land" and "by right of eminent domain" were mentioned. Woodrow Larkin brought up where the waterline would fall once the valley was flooded and Digger quickly figured it was just about level with Addie. Then Ward Smith rose. "This is the list," he said, unofficial of course, the list of those within the town of Pepacton living under the projected waterline. As each name and place was mentioned, men shifted, women gripped their purses.

At the end, Sims rose and spread his palms outward. "Let us now bow our heads in prayer."

Digger would not lower his head. Was Sims speaking for the Lord? Maybe that's why God said His name should not be spoken, lest he who spoke it confused Him with his own bloated self.

"In this dreadful news we've heard here today we find God's teaching . . . Can I say something radical?" Sims paused. "God promises us a community, and His community transcends this land we farm, this fertile valley. In His wondrous light, His *community* cannot be extinguished."

Digger got up to leave. Three rows back, Peg Bridges was already gone.

Digger had been close to Sims once. They had each loved the same thing, first alone and then together they loved it, dearly. It was the summer of 1924 when Sims arrived, Thomas Sims from the Middle West, with his easy smile. Often in the mornings, the reverend's Chevrolet would be parked by Digger's barn. Sims was the same age as Digger (though rounder and shorter), and like Digger, he'd memorized a store of scripture.

The reverend was married and had a new congregation to care for, but he followed Digger as he did his chores. Sims would recite a psalm, then Digger would.

He raiseth the poor out of the dust,
and lifteth the needy out of the dunghill.

Digger had never known another man as engaged with the Book as he'd been for so many solitary years. When Digger was a boy, his pa was either off the farm working or too sick with consumption, leaving his ma to take on extra work, the townspeople's laundry or their mending. His grandma too was worked to the bone. His grandpa—the one he was closest to— had mainly practical interests. Digger was left to reading the one book in the house, a book full of stories, the same ones Sims grew up on. Digger started inviting the reverend into the kitchen for coffee, and eventually decided to walk into his church. "A church virgin," Sims called him.

Digger hadn't thought he was lonely. But his grandpa had died the year before and then his ma lay dying with a brain tumor. After the doctor started administering morphine, her last intelligible sentence was, "I dreamed we were havin' a big celebration and everyone was gittin' along." She lost the ability to answer his simple questions—Are you cold? Want another pillow?—and would look up at him with a scared or worried face. She'd never been affectionate, but now she puckered her lips into a kiss whenever he had to leave the room. So Digger looked forward to Sims's visits. If it was evening, he'd pour two glasses of whiskey, and they sat facing the bed as if facing a fire.

One evening, Sims broke the silence. "My real mother was just sixteen when she had me. Been on the street already a few years."

Digger nodded. "Well, looks like she raised you right."

Sims shook his head. "I had nothing, not even a last name. But a young couple from Galesburg, Illinois, found me one day stealing scraps from back of a store and took me on. Took me back to Galesburg and I never saw my natural mother again. Yes, Helen and Edward Sims, they raised me, sent me to school for the first time. I was eight years old and had never gone to school. The other children, they'd often tease—especially an older boy named Louis Parker, he called me bastard-child. I ran home from school crying one day and my stepdad, he said, 'You'll always be a son to me, Thomas.' He said that, he did. Then he dedicated me to the Lord." Sims shook his fist and shouted, "Through the Mercy of the Lord Jesus Christ!"

The shout made Digger uneasy—even his ma's head twisted a bit—but he nodded anyway, wanting to accommodate his new friend and the full breadth of his story. That night, Sims prayed while Digger watched his ma's breath, something he did continually without thinking.

Weeks later she died, and Sims was there to give her a final blessing. Then he sat and waited while Digger held on to her arm as she grew cold. After a while they sat at the kitchen table and drank whiskey. It wasn't too long before Sims started to sing.

Return unto thy rest, O my soul
For He hath delivered thee from death,
Mine eyes from tears, and my feet from falling.
I will walk before the Lord in the land of the living.

It was a psalm Digger loved and Sims sang it and others for hours. Listening to Sims's voice, Digger cried. His mother was his final link, and no one was left between him and the cliff at the end.

Peg was halfway to the creamery when Digger pulled the truck over. Only about an inch of snow had fallen, but it looked like it could turn into something, the flakes getting smaller and heavier.

"Well, well," she said, smiling as she climbed in.

He saw her coat had no buttons left and she was wearing only a scarf for her head. She brushed the snow off her sleeves. He hadn't seen her in close to a year but it never felt that long with Peg. Same dark eyes, though they looked a little tired. And the same hips too, swinging loosely when she walked, like the saddle horses she had grown up with until her daddy ran off and one by one they all got sold.

"Goin' home?" he asked, pulling onto the road again.

"I can," she said, turning to him. "You don't look good, Will."

He shook his head, suddenly he couldn't speak. Luckily, with Peg he didn't have to. He had known her since he was twelve and she was in the first grade. They were both walking to school on the River Road, he was behind but catching up when a bear ran out from the Whittaker farm right toward them. He realized then that Peg was eating out of her lunch bag and he grabbed a branch from the side of the road, leapt in front of her, and held the bear off till Ed's father came out and shot him. But he never made it to school that day to tell the story because he had soiled his pants. He knew Peg knew but she always kept his secret. And for that he'd often hand her a penny when he saw her or give her an apple or cookie from his lunch.

"What's on your mind, Will?"

He shook his head.

She laid her hand on his arm. "I'm so sorry about Addie."

"She might be under the—" He swallowed.

"Don't even try," she said and patted him.

You could say anything you wanted to about Peg Bridges, but she was a queen and always had been. Tenderness. Tenderness was her territory. What the town talked about most were the fatherless children, two, maybe three by now, each one given to a childless couple.

"You ain't ever been simple, have you?" she said.

"A few times." He could breathe again now, looking out over the white road.

She let out a little laugh and pulled at his coat. "Durin' your lessons."

Only Peg could make him blush. After Addie had yelled *Stop!* that night in the rented room and he couldn't face her again for weeks, he'd gone to Peg and confessed. "Ah, Will," she had said, "you finally got yourself a woman right for you, and everybody knows that ain't been easy. And all you need now is some old-fashioned learnin'. Just like you done in school. But this time you don't get a primer, you get me." And she spread her arms. "We'll go step by step. You got to get used to it, very used to it," she said as her fingers traveled across his skin. It was like having bugs let loose all over him, bugs and fire too, the heat going straight down and pushing up through his pants. "I'm goin' closer now," she'd say, "closer to your heart," undoing the buttons on his shirt. He was breathing so hard and she kept repeating in her calm, sweet voice, "Just roll it under—plow it under." It took him five lessons in all, three before he lasted more than an instant.

He turned up Bussy Hollow Road. Peg still lived at home with her blind, seventy-year-old mother.

"This here is Willis Benton, Ma. Remember Will?" Peg said in a very low voice as she opened the kitchen door. The house smelled like coal, corn bread, burned maple syrup. Digger couldn't believe her mother could hear Peg, sitting on the far side of the kitchen by the stove, but she nodded in their direction. "I know Willis," she said, her mouth with no teeth opening and closing like a little bird's, "the one just lost his wife." She was wrapped in one of her bright red-and-yellow afghans she'd crocheted. Peg opened the stove, poured in half a scuttle of coal, then tilted her head toward an inside door, "Come on back."

They walked through a room filled with boxes to the bedroom. Peg slept in the same bed as her mother—to get her to the chamber pot in time and to make sure her ma didn't die on her, she said, grinning. It reminded Digger of her main lesson. You got to ride yourself like you ride a horse, she'd told him, how you never let a horse run through your hand, but you never let him die under you, neither, you don't let him give out.

Giving out, that's what he was doing now. He took off his coat, laid down on the rumpled bed, his boots hanging off the edge. "I can't do it, Peg. Can't go on."

"Of course you can, Will." She sat down next to him and put her hand against his cheek. "How long has it been since you slept?"

He shook his head again.

"I think you need a little nap." She stroked his shirt pocket.

He closed his eyes but as soon as he felt himself sinking into sleep, becoming more and more alone, he started, afraid.

"Easy, easy now," she said.

"I can't do it," he said a few times.

She put her palm on his forehead, brushed back his hair. He opened his eyes, lifted his forefinger toward her chest.

"Can I?"

"Why of course. What do you think I got them for, my mother?" She smiled as she unbuttoned her blouse. "Ah, Will . . . you need a little peek?"

Her arms were still skinny and very white like when she was a girl, and while she was unhooking her brassiere, her elbows out to the side, he saw the two moles near her underarms. Like old friends. He'd been so stunned by them once and by the intimacy of a woman's skin, the nearness of it undoing him. As her brassiere lowered, her breasts did too, they kept on lowering, they were even bigger than he remembered, those times he had traced each stretch mark, which headed, always, straight toward the nipple. Like running logs down a river, he'd said. It was maybe his third or fourth lesson.

He took a deep breath, leaned back, and closed his eyes. "I thank you, Peg. You're a generous woman."

She laughed. "You're the strangest man, do you know that?"

"Oh, I've been tormented. More lately."

"You don't want a little feel, Will?"

He lifted his head and looked at her breasts as if he had to answer a very hard question. He raised his right hand and then dropped it again. "Not this time . . . I don't think . . . not this time." And he lay back on the pillow again. She pulled a blanket up over her shoulders and covered herself.

"Now, then, you just drift off to sleep," she said, patting him on the chest. "It's gonna be alright." Her voice got quieter and quieter, though he could still feel the weight of her hand as the dark washed over him.

Later, driving home through the snow, Digger said to himself, I'm a condemned man on a soon-to-be-condemned farm, but truth was he felt much better. He had slept.

The river froze. Hay was laid up along the foundation of every house, and the last cows were brought in for the winter. Signs of Christmas appeared—wreaths, red ribbons, pinecones and greens wired up with berries, the rehearsing of carols. It was unbearable. In the evenings, Leenie braided crowns of princess pine for her sisters.

He wouldn't go to her family's home, he couldn't. He'd drop her and Rebecca off on Christmas Eve and pick them up the next evening. He'd send another carload of groceries.

While Leenie braided, he sat at the other end of the table under his own light, poring over his grandfather's maps. The next afternoon he put on his snowshoes and headed up to Addie's grave, tracking a new contour where the waterline would fall. No matter how many times he went, he was always taken aback when he came upon her rock. The wave of snow blown from the ridge stopped just shy of the spot and bent gracefully down to her. He stood for a long time. Where there had been the sharp stab of loss, or cold, or numbness, he felt now love dispersing.

On his way home he spotted Leenie walking with Rebecca downriver under the line of elms; he watched her from the upper field. She turned by the mudflats and walked to where an eddy scooped the shore into the shape of a quarter-moon. The snow near the river was crusty and windblown, she could walk right over it. Holding Rebecca close, she squatted near the water. What was she doing? Punching a hole through the thin ice? Suddenly she stood and headed back. He wanted to run home and ask her questions. He had never even asked her about the pregnant mare. He would sit with her and talk. He could tell her how his mother raised him alone on the farm while his father worked on the railroad. He felt the old sadness creep in—from the day when, fourteen years old and his father sick with consumption, he walked out of his mother's kitchen intending to leave the farm, to leave his aging grandfather to work it by himself—on his way to Pennsylvania as if the name meant something to him, and his ma didn't cry or say a word but handed him a satchelful of bread, some ham, and two jars. He walked seventeen miles and the whole time considered that clinking glass a burden he was carrying for his ma, but then his first night holed up in a hay barn, even his grand schemes didn't seem to alleviate the darkness and he opened the jar of her raspberry jelly and cried the moment he tasted it. And the other, smaller jar filled with salt, as if his mother couldn't imagine him going to a place where he could find salt. Three months later he was back, and back to stay.

But he never did sit and talk with Leenie that night. After supper, he went out to the barn to check on—what was it—a sick cow? and when he came back in, she was already upstairs asleep in the bed.

On the first day of winter, the darkest day of the year, Digger stopped at Lloyd's after bringing his milk to the creamery. He figured he couldn't ignore Christmas any longer. Every year, the first Saturday of December the Lloyds placed a life-sized crèche in the window and every year they took it out again the second Saturday of January. But now in front of it, there was a poster taped to the glass: "Right of Eminent Domain Is Wrong" in Amanda Keller's calligraphy. It touched him, seeing the extra curls on the capital letters, but it saddened him too.

John, Uriah Lloyd's second son, was behind the counter. "Where do *you* say the water's gonna rise to, Willis?" he asked, his big tomato face smiling. John was a jovial man, friendly with his customers, and because of that no one respected him like they did Uriah.

"Below Addie's grave," Digger answered, looking straight at him. John lowered his eyes and didn't ask any more questions. It was just what Addie would complain about: his knack for ending a conversation he didn't want to have.

Digger settled up Edith's past bill and ordered the new groceries. After John wrote down each item, he nodded, signaling Digger to go on as he tried to recall what each child loved. At the end, he added licorice for Leenie. He pulled out his wallet to pay, then spotted a pyramid of oranges on a table. "When did those come in?"

"Yesterday mornin'," John answered, "up from Florida by train."

Digger ordered a box of six to be delivered to Peg Bridges and her mother. "For Christmas," he said.

John nodded, and Digger appreciated his silence. He picked up two oranges and set them on the counter. He was sure Leenie had never tasted one. "As long as I got my wallet out."

"Thank you kindly," John said.

That evening, after Leenie put Rebecca down and laced herself up, he brought out the oranges. "I bought this for you."

She looked down at his palm and started to laugh. He didn't understand. Finally, she took the orange but kept laughing.

"You have to peel it," he said.

"I know. I ain't that much hill."

"You tasted one before?"

She shook her head.

"I got one to eat too."

She stood and hurried into the parlor. He heard her sniffing and cooing as she peeled it. He grabbed the lantern off the table and walked through the door, but she ran up the stairs saying, "I can't, I can't eat it in front of you."

He stood outside her door and fought with himself. Just leave her be, let her eat it alone, for chrissakes. But he kept his hand on the knob. Finally, he opened the door and saw her sitting on the bed, her eyes closed, her mouth puckered, her fingers held up to her face holding a section, the peels and the rest of the orange in her lap. He set the light down on the bedside table. She kept chewing very slowly. *O taste and see,* wasn't that what the psalmist had said?

He watched her as she pulled each section from the orange and put it in her mouth, and though he hated himself for it, he stayed there looking as tears ran down her face.

9

On the outside everything looked normal. Monday was wash day. Tuesdays, Leenie made bread with her great-aunt's sourdough and sometimes it rose perfectly and looked like her mother's. Wednesdays, either Old Man Richard or his grandson delivered Louise's milk. Thursdays or Fridays, she received a letter from home, from Frances and Mary, always with some drawing from Janey. She spent the better part of every day making meals and here and there, when Rebecca was asleep, she cleaned some, and if the afternoons were warm enough, she beat a rug or two outdoors over the front pasture fence.

Digger still swept the kitchen floor each morning—it calmed him—and if he didn't take out his maps, he read psalms every evening, first to himself, then out loud, and then to himself again. Rebecca slowly shifted to cow's milk and though it was a gradual change, she got colic. Hettie came and they made a hammock from a sheet and swung her little body as fast as they could until she stopped crying. Every two or three days, it snowed and the paths needed to be shoveled again. When it was clear and bright, Leenie bundled up in Addie's coat, shawl, and gloves, wrapped Rebecca in a quilt, and carried her along the river where the snow was hard. Some days, the black, bare branches on the elms glistened with ice. Or the ice would fall, clattering like typewriter keys and leaving glassy half-pipes her sisters would've loved all over the ground. Outside was where words came to her the most. It wouldn't take much—a few chickens scratching up grain left by the horses, their beaks knocking against the cement—just that and: h*eart shrunk like a pellet*. It wasn't *her* heart, though, she knew that, her heart felt big and damp.

One time the word *carnal* visited her and though she knew what it meant, she looked it up in Addie's dictionary. "Sensual, material, corporeal, the seat of appetite and passion, not spiritual, fleshly." A word she could understand—it was low, like she was, like she knew she was, and it wanted to elevate itself too, coupling right there in the dictionary with the venerable word *knowledge*.

Sometime during the winter she started calling Uncle Willis Digger, without being corrected or correcting herself first. It was about the same time she started dueling with him—with words. His voice had risen again into a psalm as it had so many times when she was trying to read: "Thou hast made the earth to tremble, thou hast broken it," and she thought, enough! and answered back with the first line of Millay's "The Death of Autumn":

"When reeds are dead and a straw to thatch the marshes."

He went on, undaunted, "Heal the breaches thereof; for it shaketh."

"And over the flattened rushes."

"Purge me with hyssop."

"Stripped of its secret, open, stark and bleak, / Blackens afar the half-forgotten creek."

Then his voice rose again: "Wash me and I shall be whiter than snow!"

"Then leans on me the weight of the year!"

"That the bones which thou hast broken may rejoice!"

"I know that Beauty must ail and die!"

He was silent.

"What is the Spring to me?" she finished, thinking she had won.

But then, his voice settled, victorious: "As the hart panteth after the water brooks, so panteth my soul after thee . . . and deep calleth unto deep."

Most times he'd win, and sometimes she'd concede right away. Like when he turned to her: "When I kept silence, my bones waxed old through my roaring all the day long."

"Again," she said, lifting her head. When he repeated it, she nodded and turned back to her book.

One afternoon, Digger came back from Addie's grave earlier than usual, before Burdett arrived for the evening milk. Digger tossed his cap onto the table, walked past her by the stove—she was reading over Rebecca nursing—and up the stairs. She put her book down, heard the door to his room shut. After Rebecca finished nursing, Leenie went up and stood outside his door. He was crying. It wasn't her place to go in, but if she didn't, who was she, and what was her life here?

She walked around the bed and lay down on the quilt beside him, though he was turned away. He still had his coat on. The embroidery on the pillowcase was almost worn off—such a contrast to him, his dark messy hair and what she could see of his face. She brought her body up close behind him and held him until he stopped crying. Then she got up and went out.

Digger was a man of patterns. Most afternoons, he went to Addie's grave, and then before milking, he lay in his room and she went up.

Rebecca was often with them on the bed. Sometimes Leenie would set her facedown on Digger's stomach. He'd prop the pillow up behind his neck and watch her lift her head and bob it toward him, her arms and legs bobbing too. He held her hands.

Little by little, he talked. He said he'd made a mistake, where he laid Addie. Leenie pieced it together from what she'd read in the *Valley Gazette*.

"Would've done better," Digger said, "if I'd buried her in the cemetery. But she hated cemeteries. All the *people* in them. Being so close to all those people!" He chuckled and then stopped. "But all those graves will be saved."

She lay there next to him as dusk turned darker, the sky lowering itself to the ground. Maybe that's what night was, the sky wanting to be inside the ground. Sometimes after he got up to go milk, she stayed and watched the night roll in. She liked how close it came. Bright was far away, bright was cold.

One day in late February, after a long snowfall that didn't amount to much, little puffs on the branches out the bedroom window, she asked, "It's unmarked, isn't it? I remember that was important . . . her grave unmarked."

He nodded. "That it not be touched."

"By hands?"

"By tools, human tools. Exodus 20."

"But what about everything else then? Where we live? The farm?" She felt bold. "Anything we touch is bad? Anything we *make*?"

"Not bad, desecrated."

"Well, *desecrated* doesn't sound very good. Why are we so bad we desecrate everything we make?"

"We ain't pure."

"What's pure?"

"God. What He makes. His creation."

"What are we supposed to do with ourselves, sit around like dogs and wait? You're a funny man, Digger. You got ideas but then . . . then they *work* on you, twist you around something awful."

"I shouldn't have ideas?"

"I ain't saying that. It's just I don't understand most of yours that come from that Bible, but I don't think you do either."

"You got any ideas?"

"Sort of."

"Like what?"

"Well . . ." She was playing with Rebecca, holding the blanket near her little fingers until she grabbed it. "That we're a lot more like animals than we think we are." Rebecca took hold of the blanket, and Leenie brought her face down and kissed Rebecca's nose. "My grandma used to say, God don't love ugly."

Sometimes he told her about Addie. They'd been happy, but Digger said, "She didn't like I didn't talk much."

Leenie nodded.

Digger studied her. "You're something, you know that? You ain't been out enough to know. But a lot of people have been tamed. You're civilized, but you ain't been tamed."

The days got longer, the nights shorter. The snow was still deep but it was dirty and most of it was packed down or blown. When Digger and Burdett skidded logs in from the woods, they used the same route every time, driving the horses over the windy flat up on the knoll where all the snow was blown off. Windiest place in the valley, Digger said.

In early March, Burdett took sick, and each morning and night, Leenie helped Digger milk, moving Rebecca's basket to keep her within earshot. One evening, Rebecca started to cry and Leenie plopped her stool in the center aisle and started nursing. Digger looked over while he was milking and she looked up at the same time and they both started laughing.

She cocked her head to the side. "Am I your best cow?"

"Ah, honey, you ain't no cow," he said, turning to his work again. He was finishing off, stripping the last few squirts into the bucket. "You're . . . you're my Leenie."

A couple of weeks later, in the middle of March, one early afternoon, Leenie walked out with Rebecca to the sugar shack so she could help Digger boil syrup—mainly watch the pan, adding butter now and then to cut the foam down. She set Rebecca up with pillows on the stone shelf and stood over the evaporator, smelling the sugary steam mix with Digger's sweat. Her arms and hands and face grew sticky and the front of her dress clung to her, but her back stayed cool from the breeze coming in through the slats. The boiling sap seemed loud enough to drown out everything, except for—suddenly—a grinding noise that made her jump.

"It's just the river," Digger yelled as he shoved a log into the firebox, "the ice breakin'."

She ran outside to the low pasture, and for over an hour while the sun was high, she watched the ice crack, splintering into small countries that broke away and disappeared around the bend. By late afternoon, the river was open.

She was getting used to the river, though she was still frightened of it. Almost every winter or spring, it flooded down at Emery Crawford's, where the ice dammed up in the narrows. Once his Model A was found twelve miles down in a tangled mess of logs.

With the river open, Leenie kept her eye on the bathing spot. Frances's birthday was coming up and Leenie promised herself she would go home clean. But the weather grew cold again, the sap stopped flowing, and Leenie gave up hope of bathing any time soon.

* * *

Leenie wracked her brain trying to think of something to give to Frances. If she walked to Lloyd's for saltwater taffy, Frances would be hurt Leenie didn't do more than use Digger's money to buy it. She could make Frances a purse from Addie's sewing scraps, but she could just hear Frances thinking, "And where am *I* gonna go with a purse?"

Leenie grew more anxious as the day drew nearer, until finally, Digger said, "Why, Addie got a new coat from Alma's just before . . . You could wrap that up and give it to her—why, she'd *want* Frances to have it."

"It's spring," Leenie said.

"Well, she still needs a coat."

"Yes, she certainly does."

"I think it might be blue."

"She loves blue!"

"Might not be."

"Doesn't matter. It's a *new* coat!" Leenie clapped her hands.

While she washed the dishes, Digger rummaged through Addie's closet and brought it down, still in a box.

Leenie wiped her hands dry and opened it. Blue velour. "A boughten coat! Frances'll just die!" Then she glanced at Digger.

He didn't seem upset by the word. "We don't have to mention it was Addie bought it," he said.

On the night before she went home for Frances's birthday, Leenie rolled the tub out from the corner of the shed and pushed it up the steps through the kitchen door. The tub was much larger than the one her ma used. This one Leenie could sit in. She placed it between the sink and stove, close enough to the fire to feel the heat. Digger kept reading the psalms. Every once in a while, Rebecca fussed and he leaned down and put his hand on her until she quieted. Leenie filled the firebox with oak, got the fire burning good and hot. Three large pots of boiling water would do. The kitchen filled with steam, the inside of the windows dripping, shining from the lamps. She had just added in the cold water when Digger shut the Book and stood. He took the lantern into the landing at the top of the cellar stairs where the medicine cabinet was and came out with a small bottle he held out to her. They'd bought it in New York City, he said, the only time they'd been there.

She shook her head, no.

"But it's never been opened." Finally, she took it. *Sandalwood,* the label said.

She poured in drops of oil. The smell surrounded them, and he didn't leave. She lowered the lamp wicks until there was more shadow than light, then turned her back to him, undressed, and got in, curling as low as she could into the water.

Bits of oil shone red and purple on the surface. She heard him behind her take off his belt, his boots, his pants, his shirt, his union suit—she didn't turn around, she had never seen a man naked. She rose up and stepped out, dripping on the floor. With her back to him, she gripped the far side of the tub and bent over. He stepped off to the side, but she stepped sideways too. Finally he came up against her and grabbed her hips.

She was leaning over the water, dripping. He brought his head down near hers. "Are you cold?" he whispered. She shook her head. He poured handfuls of water over her back and shoulders. A sandalwood fog rose around them, it was a room inside a room, a room with no door. Then his right hand stopped on her breast, and his other roamed over her, lifting and spreading her cheeks, he was looking for her, but she knew it was not just *him* looking for her, it was something inhuman too—so that when the dark pole brushed past her hip and against her buttocks, she widened her feet and raised toward him until it found her.

"Does that hurt?" he asked.

"A little," she said, closing her eyes, "but don't stop." Then her feet lifted off the floor and he broke through.

10

Behold thou desireth truth in the inward parts: and in the hidden part thou shalt make me know wisdom. Grief could suddenly close his throat or steal his life force, but today life pumped through him like a fever. Leenie sat next to him in the truck, holding the baby upright on her lap and staring straight ahead.

"Is it seeing your ma?" he asked as they neared Mary Smith.

She nodded, her eyes tearing.

He didn't know what to say, so he put his hand on her knee.

"I'm just the same, though," she said. "As I was."

He nodded, "Mostly."

"I thought I'd be more . . . changed."

He smiled at her. In her face was the openness he loved. She looked out at the world, wondering. But last night, she'd wanted him with her eyes closed. His memory plucked at it, the *persistence* of her backside turning toward him; he knew there'd be more too. And now he had to face Edith.

As soon as they passed the water trough at the corner of the barn, Digger saw Leenie's father, surrounded by small, scraggly pullets, darting their heads in and out of the slop bucket he was carrying to his sow.

"Well, it's about time," Sam said, and if Leenie was surprised she didn't show it. They hugged, and Sam said, "It's mighty lonely around here without you, and I've only been home an hour." He stuck out his hand to Digger. "Willis."

"Sam."

"And I see we got one more pretty girl in this world, don't we?" Sam said, leaning toward Rebecca.

Digger smelled the liquor on him. Just home, the sun barely reaching the western sky. Sam had a beard now and looked a bit seedy but was still tall and handsome, with a wide jaw, a long, distinctive nose. The crow's-feet around his eyes welcomed in anyone he turned his attention to. It was from him Leenie got the slim grace she never lost even when she picked up a washtub. Digger had always been fond of Sam. Everyone was. Osmer said Sam could charm an extra skin off a snake. But seeing Sam's hand on Leenie's shoulder now, Digger felt revolted. He went toward the house.

The foundation still had manure banked halfway up the bottom panes of the windows. Edith wasn't going to waste any hay insulating. She was in the back corner of the kitchen wringing out a rag over a bucket of steaming water and ammonia. When she saw him, she straightened and put a hand on her hip.

"Comes home with all this fanfare. 'In time for my girl's birthday,' he says, huggin' and kissin' the children. 'April Fool's!' And now he's halfway to a drunk. Comes with nothin', of course"—she threw her hand into the air—"as if he himself was all was needed."

"I know," Digger said, feeling tender.

"Leenie down in the horse barn with him?"

Digger nodded, as Edith bent toward the floor to scrub.

"*She* don't see any of the mess he makes. Probably down there gloatin' over the pregnant mare together." She wrung out the rag. Her hands were a deep red. "They're both of 'em nothin' but dreamers, Willis."

"Leenie's got a head on her shoulders, Edith."

"Why we got to git her to hu-minities school. Where they can load her up with books. Surround her with her own kind." She looked at him. She probably did love Leenie after all, or would, if she had the time. "How *you* holdin' up, Willis?"

"Some days are better than others." Out the window, the wall of manure steamed in the late-afternoon sun.

Leenie came up to the house, and he saw her awkwardness as she leaned in and kissed her mother's cheek. "Hi, Mama."

"Don't step over there. It's still sticky. I'm heatin' another pot." Edith was a great believer in scalding-hot water. "Janey spilled the honey she was warmin' seems everywhere. We was givin' it to Emma."

"She coughin'?"

"Just awful. Janey's watchin' over her upstairs."

"And Mary? Frances?"

"They're down milkin'. At least I hope they started, since your father's already . . . We was plannin' an early supper."

"Whatta you want me to do?" Leenie asked.

Her ma's mouth quivered slightly. "Bless your heart, girl." If this woman could cry, she'd cry now, Digger thought. "Why don't you help Frances out, it ain't been a good day for her."

Leenie turned and almost ran out the door. Digger understood: work was shelter—work outside their mother's territory, work they couldn't make a mistake at.

"I'll get right on Osmer's car," he said, wanting to leave himself. It had been drained for the winter and he'd sent her word through Richard that he'd get it running come spring.

"Well, don't let Sam git his hands into it."

* * *

Lazy lay in front of the Model T, and Sam leaned against the car talking to Digger's feet sticking out from under it.

"Still git parts for that Larrabee?" Sam asked.

"Yut."

"Up north, they can't git 'em," Sam said. "Say the whole company's goin' bankrupt."

"Billy Holt over in Downsville—he got two old parts trucks he keeps in back. Well, well, here they are." Digger found the transmission bands that had come loose. He was starting to see better in the darkness. "Sorry things they are, but we'll get 'em tightened up here while we're at it."

"You know that fella Murphy?" Sam asked. "Lives down near Jack where the crick crosses over, in that hole there?"

"Yut."

"Used to be quite a gui-tar player." Sam was easing into a story. For every bit of story, he took in a swallow of whiskey.

"Murphy loved moonshine somethin' awful, but he's gotten chummy with the reverend. Like you used to be. Right, Willis?"

Digger wasn't going to fall into that trap. People's lives were Sam's fodder.

Sam laughed. "Shut up tight as a drum, ain't ya, Willis? But Murphy, they say he's been enraptured by the Lord Jesus Christ, and he's gone dry. Seems to be required if you're one of Sims's boys."

"Sims likes his whiskey," Digger said.

"Well, Murphy went to Jimmy's with another man. Had a crowbar and a sledge. They smashed the barrels, the pipes, the cooker, the windows in the shed, everything."

"That doesn't sound like Sims."

"It don't? You and him still friends?"

"Too long a story, Sam."

"We don't got time? All we got around here is time. Not a stitch of work except for Kolb's. I hear he's picked up another acid factory—the one used to be the tannery in Shinhopple, before the hemlocks were all taken." Sam shook his head. "Yut, *he* got plenty of money. Almost had a mind to sign up there. Till I heard 'bout Jimmy."

Digger didn't believe loyalty to Jimmy kept Sam from work. "I hear Kolb's givin' out free suppers to his workers," Digger said. "Every Sunday night. And their families too."

"Free suppers?" Sam shook his head. "Give your men fifteen, twenty dollars a week all used up at the company store and then make 'em grateful for a free supper." Sam laughed. "Peg's been run off, Will. And don't tell me that ain't got Sims writ all over it."

It was not so much Sims himself, but his mission that had driven Digger away and inadvertently toward Peg. After Digger's mother had died and Sims had gone home, Digger sat at the kitchen table with a pen and the family Bible open to the records page. In his great-grandma's hand, faded to gray, was written:

Elbert Benton, born March 31, 1844

Then, in blue ink, his grandma's writing of her marriage:

Sarah Thompson married to Elbert Benton, September 21, 1867

Then his pa's birth:

William Benton, born January 4, 186

The 8 at the end had been written in pencil and then rubbed out—along with some of the shame. He touched the erasure. All the years that fact had kept his family from the Church. Digger shook his head.

Five children followed his pa, though two died young. Down the page his mother's handwriting recorded his own beginnings:

Nettie Whitcomb married to William Benton, July 7, 1888
Willis John Whitcomb Benton, born June 6, 1889

Then came his baby sister, who never got a chance at life:

Lily Benton, born January 23, 1894, died May 2, age 3 mos.

His pa's, grandma's, and grandpa's deaths were recorded. Below them, he carefully wrote:

Nettie Benton, died September 17, 1924

That afternoon Digger sat in the back pew of Sims's church. He was there at choir practice so he could hear the reverend sing again. Digger's pa, the illegitimate child, was long dead, but Digger still wasn't at ease in the large room with its high ceiling. *It was* them *picked the battle,* his grandpa had said. *They're the ones drew the line.*

Entering a church wasn't his first betrayal of Elbert Benton. Digger had bought a tractor, which his grandpa said would steal moisture from the earth.

When Sims asked Digger to stay to hear a sermon rehearsal, he felt grateful enough for the reverend's watch over his ma's deathbed to oblige.

Sims read from Romans 8: "For we are saved by hope: but . . .

we know not what we should pray for as we ought: the Spirit itself maketh intercession for us . . . all things work together for good to them that love God, to them who are called according to His purpose.

"The Book tells us," Sims said, "that we know *not* what we should pray for. And so we are frightened when our ship is blown off course. We wonder, *Where has gone our purpose?*" He looked back and forth across the empty pews.

"You will not be able to find His purpose"—he threw his arm forward with each phrase—"in that which befalls you, in the setback that disappoints you, or the loss that pains you . . ."

Digger understood the sermon was intended for him and deliberately from the New Testament. Sims knew his bias against it, but what farmer could disagree with finding purpose in what was laid before him?

"Yet the Word of the Lord offers great comfort." Sims swept his eyes across the church. "Not all that happens in life is good, but all things *work together* for good to Them That Love God."

Digger didn't like that at all, he didn't want God to come closer. He was where He should be. And why would God even care if He was loved? You could love the sun, Digger certainly did, but would it *care?* Would it stop shining on you if you didn't love it? He shook Sims's hand before he left, but Digger knew he could not join his church.

Sims still dropped by two or three times a week. "My wrestling partner," the reverend called him after one of their philosophical discussions. But after the night Addie yelled *Stop!* Digger paid *him* a visit.

Sitting in the parsonage kitchen, he told Sims everything he did and wanted to do with the woman he loved, and how lonely he'd been for years. Sims stood and laid his hands upon Digger's head, praying to God to ease his tormented soul. Sims's voice was soothing, but after a while Digger heard the words the reverend was saying. "It is only his lust, Jesus, that hardens him now against receiving Thy merciful love." Digger felt the pressure of Sims's palm upon his head, and he gathered himself in from the room, like a river reversing course.

"Willis Benton—a good man, an earnest man—now at this precious time, will you take the Lord Jesus Christ as your personal Savior?" Digger stood and Sims backed up. "Will, Will, come on. She's a temptress, don't you see? They all are."

As Digger headed for the door, Sims's voice went hard. "If you walk out now, Benton, don't you ever come back and waste my precious time."

Digger left and drove to Peg's house and Peg took him into the bedroom and began his lessons.

Sam was up and down all through supper. He always kept a flask in his chest pocket, but never drank in front of his girls. Even six-year-old Janey glared as he walked out the door. Edith had done the best she could with nothing fresh but ramps she'd loaded into a fried hash made with cured venison.

Leenie had brought fourteen candles, plus one to grow on. Mary and Janey arranged them into an *F* on the applesauce cake, which Edith made because Frances didn't like cakes with icing. Sam and Mary sang "Happy Birthday," Mary doing the harmony. She was the only one who got Sam's beautiful voice. Everyone else just hummed.

After the cake, Sam mumbled, "Gonna go use God's bathroom," and headed for the door. Frances was opening Leenie's present.

"I can't believe it," Frances said, staring down into the box, "a boughten coat." She lifted it out—blue velour with a fur collar and sateen lining. "Is it from Alma's store?"

Leenie nodded. Frances put it on and twirled around.

"We know who paid for that coat."

Frances stopped. Leenie lowered the lantern, set it back on the table.

"*I* didn't," Digger said.

"Well, then, who did?"

"Oh, come on, Edith, let 'em be," Sam said, standing in the doorway. "Frances, that's a coat you can wear right to town, and I don't mean Pepacton." He chuckled, the flask still in his hand. Then he went back out.

Edith cleared the plates and set them on the side of the stove by the two pots of hot water. Mary, as if on cue, went over and put the dirty dishes, one by one, in the bigger pot, the silverware in the smaller. Leenie held Rebecca against her chest, bouncing in place. "Now, don't *you* start fussin'," she whispered into her ear.

"Leenie, it's just beautiful." Frances lowered her voice. "I don't care who bought it, it's you picking it out that counts."

"I was a little worried about the arms but it fits you just right," Leenie said.

Frances brushed her hand over the sleeve. "I never thought I'd have my own coat."

"It's Addie's coat." Edith turned toward the table. "Ain't it, Willis?"

"No, Edith, that one never was." He got up and looked at Leenie. She nodded.

"Bye, Ma," Leenie said, giving her a kiss that didn't quite reach her cheek. As the sisters hugged each other, they heard their father singing in the yard.

Land where my fathers died,
Land of the pilgrims' pride
From every mountainside . . .

A week later Leenie received a thick envelope from her sisters. Janey had sent a picture she'd drawn of herself, her eyes with lines running straight down to show tears. Frances wrote a letter saying the day after her birthday their daddy had gone to get work at the acid factory in Shinhopple. The first paycheck wouldn't come for a week, but they were already living large (*HA!* Frances wrote in the margin). Mama was making new dresses for them with material Mrs. Kolb gave out at the company store.

Sam had been right about Peg being gone. Her blind mother had been taken to Liberty and put in a home filled with TB patients. Digger wanted to find out where Peg was, so he took a ride up to Jimmy's. The kitchen door was open, but Jimmy wasn't there. Digger walked up Jump Hill to where the still had been and into what was left of the shed; even the malt was scattered. He drove home over Close Hollow on the slim chance he'd find Peg walking. But then early the next morning, she showed up.

"Don't light any lanterns," Digger said to Leenie. He'd wrapped a quilt around Peg's shoulders. Her teeth were chattering and her lips were blue.

Holding Rebecca, Leenie filled the kettle and set it on the stove. She put a bottle of cow's milk into a pan of water and pushed it to the side burner to warm. Then she sat and waited. A watched pot. She'd give Peg plain hot water like her ma always did for cold. Just as it started to steam, she poured a cup and helped Peg bring it to her lips.

"Thank you for your kindness," Peg said. She had walked from Jimmy's brother's house up on Beech Hill. Eleven miles, Digger reckoned, going the back way. Peg's legs were crossed and Leenie saw that the outside heel of her shoe was worn off and the seams had come apart.

A thought came to Leenie that this woman who was so pretty and had such beautiful teeth was Pretty Margaret, the woman her ma hated, a woman her father had taken presents to. And Digger knew her too.

Rebecca fussed and Leenie took clean clothes from a dresser by the parlor door, and started to change her.

"Leenie, you been here since Addie died? Bless her heart," Peg said.

Leenie had a diaper pin in her mouth. "Digger, I mean Uncle Willis, is gonna send me to college. In exchange. Soon as Rebecca's old enough."

"Digger?" Peg said. "You calling yourself Digger?"

"Yut," he said.

"How in heaven's did you come up with that?"

"It was what my ma called me as a boy."

Peg sighed. "Look at that baby. She looks like Addie."

Leenie nodded. "Her mouth. But when she frowns she looks like him."

Peg smiled. "Her daddy's a very serious man."

Leenie smiled back. "If you hold her, I'll cook up some biscuits."

After they ate, Digger went out to the barn to help Burdett with the chores. Leenie poured more coffee into Peg's cup. "I've known Will since we was children," Peg said. "He saved me from a big old bear."

Leenie smiled. "A bear?"

"He was just as serious then as he is now. He seemed to know about everythin' . . . except for girls. You could tell the girls he liked 'cause soon as he'd see them, he'd walk the other way. And I was so much younger, I was maybe nine, ten years old, but Come on! I'd say. There's a dance. Take her. Ask her. But oh, he'd just twist and squirm. So I said to him once, Maybe it's better you stick with cows. And he got so hurt. He didn't like me teasin' like that."

"So Addie was his first?"

Peg paused. "His first true love, yes. And now I see you're very special to him."

"It's hard to explain," Leenie said.

"Well, love does what it does. And you have this child here, you two."

They would eat supper early, and then Digger would drive Peg to stay with Uncle Norbert, Leenie's father's brother, in Liberty. Instead of taking the truck, they'd take Wayne Stone's car. When Peg asked Digger if he was sure it would be alright to use their car, his answer was simple, they were neighbors. Leenie hadn't grown up with any neighbors, and her mother, being poor, couldn't do for others, and being proud, she didn't want them doing for her. Peg could stay at Norbert's—he was a confirmed bachelor—until she could find work.

When the clock chimed four, Leenie went upstairs to wake Peg, napping with the baby, but she was already up, kissing Becca's belly and making her laugh. Peg was wearing a skirt sewn from the same faded green feed sacks from Hanford Mills that Leenie's ma used, with the flowered print they started making a few years back, knowing their sacks were being fashioned into clothes.

"We got one hungry girl here," Peg said.

Leenie sat down on the bed, unbuttoned her blouse, and spread open her binder. Peg's eyes widened. "What in heaven's name? You don't have an ordinary brassiere?"

Leenie shook her head.

"My Lord, honey, how that must hurt."

"Only a little."

Peg got up and went to her bag. "I got one with hooks down the front that will do. Here, put it on. This girl will wait just a little longer, won't ya?" She took Rebecca and bounced her against her shoulder as Leenie stood, took off her blouse and binder and tried on Peg's brassiere. It had sateen straps and was made of the prettiest pink coutil, but though it was tailored down to her waist and had elastic panels on the sides, it was way too big.

"I can take it in around the middle," Peg said. "It's the cup size you can't help. But here, you nurse while I get some pins. Where'd Addie keep 'em?"

Leenie pointed. "She's got a whole sewin' room—and a machine too." She took off the brassiere and wrapped a blanket around her.

Peg came back and pinned the side seams while Leenie nursed.

"Even with all my sisters, I never knew a child this close. I mean from the start, a baby."

"I never had a sister," Peg said.

"My sisters, we talked all the time."

Peg stood up. "Here, try this. I can't take in much more. If it fits alright, I'll cut out the extra when I sew it up."

Rebecca wasn't happy giving up the nipple, but Peg took her anyway and watched Leenie. "Still a little big," Peg said, "but it'll do. My my, girl, you could break a cold man into a sweat."

Leenie blushed, grabbed the old binder from the bed. "Let's burn it in the stove."

The road was muddy as Digger turned Wayne's Model A onto Cat Hollow, going the back way to Norbert's in Liberty. It was raining hard, a heavy April rain coming in sideways, as much up from the ground as down from the sky. He could barely see, the rain pelting like sleet, the rhythmic clearing of the wind-shield lasting only a moment. If they had been in his truck, he would've had to pull onto the shoulder to wait out the storm, but these were the new vacuum wipers and as long as he didn't keep his foot to the floor up a hill, they didn't quit. The night closed in to their unrelenting thump thump, and the sadness welling up in Peg.

"I just couldn't do it, Will. I'd come home thinkin' the place was gonna be on fire. You couldn't tell *her* not to make corn bread!"

"I know."

"And then after she fell, I couldn't lift her. She became like deadweight."

"You done the best you could, Peg. No one took care of their mother better'n you did."

"And then once I seen I was gonna lose the house . . ."

Digger waited to hear about Sims—running her out, as Sam said—but she didn't say anything more. She swept her hair back behind her ear. "I must be a sorry sight."

"Not to me."

"One good thing, at least—I can visit her. It ain't far from Norbert's, is it?"

"Ten minutes, maybe."

"Blessings everywhere, I guess." She smiled. "If you look small enough."

Norbert opened the door wearing a wine-colored robe with a satin collar, a corded belt tied high at his waist. He was hand-some, like his brother Sam, but clean shaven, with paler skin and delicate features. His short hair was slicked back as if he'd just been to the barber.

"Glad you made it, I was getting nervous."

Peg shook Norbert's hand. They'd never met before. Digger gave Norbert Peg's suitcase and turned to leave.

"Don't you want some coffee before you head back?"

Digger shook his head. "Keeps up like this, the road will be washed." He touched Peg's elbow. "I'll send word."

Peg squeezed Digger's arm, the two men nodded, and the door closed.

Late that night, Digger came home and crawled into bed and reached for her. She was awake and surprised him by turning up the wick. She wanted to see him, all of him, and took him in her hand. It was more than she expected. She thought the very living thing was not only part of Digger, but of God, too, as if God fell from the sky and shattered into millions of shards. But no, they were not shards, not splinters of Him at all. They were divinities all their own and what she held was a dear god with its own heart. She knew she had just thrown onto her pile of wrongs one she could not recover from, but there it was, small enough to fit inside yet large enough to give warmth, closeness, sweetness, and something strong too, a dignity—yes, this could give dignity to even Monday, wash day.

11

The next afternoon, Sims paid Digger a visit. "I see the river's not behaving too badly right here," Sims said.

"Lucky this time."

"Emery lost quite a few head, didn't he?"

"Eight," Digger said.

Sims patted the face of the cow Digger was tending. "I was very sorry about your wife, Willis. I was remiss not coming by after. Shouldn't let our conflicting philosophies get in the way of our friendship, should we?"

"What can I do for you, Reverend?"

"I have a vision, Willis. One I share with my congregation. Occasionally, as a responsible leader, I have to keep an eye out for evil lurking in the shadows. The idea of evil is not one you take to, is it?"

"Probably not as you do."

"I'm a simple person, Willis. Satan sends out seeds of destruction, and they plant themselves in the fertile soil of human nature. Good is what brings God's love flowing through the community."

"Good like excludin' people lived here their whole lives?"

"I know what you're alluding to, and I'm sorry about it. I had nothin' to do with it. Some of my more zealous followers got carried away. I consider it a mistake. But the Lord has a way of making good from bad. There's been a lot less drunkenness since Jimmy's been out of business."

"And Peg?"

"Peg Bridges? I had nothing to do with whatever has befallen her. But certainly with less drunkenness comes less lasciviousness."

Digger moved toward the open barn door and Sims followed. Leenie, in Addie's red coat, was pushing the baby carriage into the driveway. She waved.

"Well, who's that?" Sims said.

"My niece."

Sims watched her roll the carriage across the lawn. "She lives here?"

Digger nodded. "Takes care of the baby."

Sims rubbed the back of his neck. "Sam's daughter."

Digger nodded.

"You best be careful, Willis. The flesh does not satisfy for long."

The earth would have to dry out some more before Digger could plow. It wouldn't have bothered his grandpa, since the moon wouldn't be new for another five days. Digger didn't pay attention to such signs, but he noted when his own timing agreed and when it didn't. He remembered the day—he was five or six—when his grandpa corrected him. "We don't call it dirt," he said, "we call it soil." It was like addressing a grown man as Mister. He looked up then at his grandfather's hand resting on top of Blue's poll, he wasn't even holding the gelding by the reins. Sometimes his grandpa would drop his hand to his side, not touch the horse at all, and Blue would still walk everywhere he did, even if his grandpa weaved about. So that evening Digger thought he'd try it too and when he led the gelding out to pasture, he threw the rope over Blue's neck and reached his little arm up toward his head. Of course Blue ran off and what a time they had catching him. But at supper, when his grandpa found out the horse hadn't pulled or shied, that his grandson had let the lead go himself, he laughed and slapped his thigh. "Moral is," he finally said, "you should never emulate me."

Five days later, as the new moon came, the ground was dry enough for spring planting. Digger hitched the plow to the tractor. The soil was thawed, but cold enough to break just right under the blade. Every spring, he came upon something he didn't want, and this spring was no different. By the oak where barbed wire had been nailed in again and again, the fence separating pasture from cornfield was down. From the toolbox on the fender, he took wire cutters, staples, a roll of wire, and spliced the fence. With luck it would last till fall.

He resumed plowing, taking comfort in the rows that advanced on the contours of his land like a regiment, ready and orderly.

The next day Digger changed the plow for the harrow and took his same circular path until the deep furrows were erased and every bit of ground was chewed soft. The repetition he hated as a boy when he followed the horses, he loved now. The fog finished rising off the river and turned westward, and the sour smell of the river after a hard spring rain floated in on the breeze.

That evening Leenie handed him the *Valley Gazette* as he sat down to supper. The headline read:

DAMMING DELAWARE RIVER APPROVED

The next morning, May first, Digger couldn't find the will to plant. He scooped the sorghum in his hand, let it fall back in the sack. Or the next day either. Finally, Burdett hitched up Dan and Johnny to the corn planter—Digger hadn't yet changed the hitch over to the tractor—and poured the kernels into the hopper.

They were being shoved into the ground too deeply at first, over three inches, until Digger stopped him and adjusted the setting to half that. He nodded to Burdett who, having done his job, turned and walked back to the barn. Each time the hopper was empty, Digger poured in another bag and forced himself on. But when the planter stuck, he didn't poke out the sod in the shoot with the wire he kept twisted around the front bar. Instead, he left the two horses standing in the field swatting mayflies and walked onto the road, down to the cemetery, past the leafless hydrangeas to his grandfather's grave.

Digger sat on the damp ground by the grave. He and his grandpa had been an odd pair: a fifty-seven-year-old illiterate Civil War veteran and a slim twelve-year-old boy who loved to read, though there was only one book in the house.

He was Willis or Will to his grandpa and grandma and to Addie and the town. He was Digger to his mother and now to himself and Leenie. But if he couldn't stand upon his land and farm it, who was he? As a youngster, he was often frightened while the crops were growing because he thought of them as fragile. He understood how large his grandpa was, able to take it all—the winds, the droughts, the floods, even a tornado ripping the roof off the south edge of the barn—feeling it all and still working each day.

Digger looked at his hands, turning them over to stare at his empty palms. His grandpa didn't speak, but the ground did. It held him up. There was timothy and clover to load in the seeder, and wheat and sorghum to plant. For it was spoken in Genesis: *While the earth remaineth, seed time and harvest.*

The day after he finished planting, Digger let the cows out. They'd spent the winter shut up in the barn and milling around in the small muddy yard, where they could drink from the river. Digger and Leenie followed them up the back lane. Over the years, Digger had made it a habit to sit on the rock pile by the gate and watch for the half hour or so it took for them to settle down. That was why he asked Leenie to leave Rebecca's basket in the barn with Burdett and walk with him up the lane.

"Dairymen's meetin' Tuesday," he said, looking straight ahead, though Leenie sat above him. "I want you to come with me."

Her knees were up and apart, making her skirt spread out like a fan. She picked mud from the hem. "At the Grange?"

"At Jack Bryant's. It's not the normal monthly meetin'. It'll be just a few of us—the lower-river farms." He peeled a blade of grass from its stem like he'd first done as a boy. "Gonna be wives there."

"I ain't a wife."

"You never said *ain't* much before you come here."

"At home I did. I just wouldn't say it out where it mattered." She tossed her hand up. "It's a feelin'—*ain't.*"

"Meetin's gonna be about the dam."

"I ain't a farmer either."

Digger didn't ask again, but Leenie said later at supper, "I don't have anythin' to wear."

"Can you make one of Addie's dresses fit?"

She looked at him and nodded. "Sometimes I feel her real close to me."

He stood and went out to the ash logs behind the barn and

picked up the maul. He drove the wedge into a block and started slamming it.

Fifteen years old. Though Addie was only twenty-five herself, twenty-one when she married him, and he thirty-seven, no young man, as the whole town was aware. Leenie was like a sister to Addie really, younger by ten years; Addie was a full nine years Edith's junior. But even with all his figuring, he couldn't get around the plain fact: Leenie was a girl yet. Shame and desire bound themselves together and overtook him, overtook even the love he felt; they burned in him and he swung harder and faster until, full of sweat and out of breath, he threw the maul down by the woodpile, staggered out to the river, took off his clothes, and jumped in.

Leenie was waiting up for him in the rocker when he came back with water seeping through his clothes.

"You alright?"

He hovered over the stove. "I can't keep away from you."

"I don't want you to."

"You're just a girl."

"I *ain't* a girl. And I don't like you thinkin' I'm one."

"But I'm—"

"I know exactly. Forty-two years next month—your birth's written in your Bible there."

"And you're fifteen."

"I'll be sixteen in three weeks."

"A child yet."

"Haven't I earned nothin'?"

"We can't just ignore how young you are—"

"You don't think I feel every single moment my youth, my silly—" She broke down crying.

"Shames me," he said. "Just shames me that I can't face the mornin', not one small chore, without knowin' you're behind me."

Leenie looked up through her tears. "What's so horrible about that?"

"What if you get pregnant?"

She wiped her nose with the back of her hand, then nodded.

"We didn't wanna think of that, did we?" he said.

"Still don't."

"You wouldn't wanna marry me, would ya?"

"I wanna go to college," she said and broke down crying again.

"You should. I know you should. I'm sorry. I just don't know how to carry on."

The mists were rising off the eddies when Digger and Leenie walked onto the Back River Road. The leaves hadn't budded yet and the red blossoms of the soft maples shone. He was carrying Rebecca. Leenie carried a tin of biscuits. She was wearing Addie's blue dress she'd taken in the night before.

"That looks nice on you," Digger said.

She smiled. "I've never been much at sewin'."

They turned up the Bryants' walk leading to the kitchen, alongside a clump of Lillian's daffodils. Jack had a Delco in the shed, its gas engine muffled by the exhaust system sticking out the back.

"My my, child, how you growed up," Lillian said. "Look just like your father."

Leenie smiled, kissed her on the cheek.

"Just set that down by the ham. Hello, Willis. And look at who we got here." Rebecca turned her face into Digger's coat. "Come on in, Will. We're waitin' on Jake and Don yet."

The wives were gathered around an electric lightbulb hanging on a cord from the ceiling. Lillian resumed the conversation. "But once I seen how much the iron took, I stopped usin' it. The radio, though, that don't take much at all."

Digger handed Rebecca to Leenie and walked into the dark parlor. The men exchanged greetings. Henry the socialist was the only one who didn't own a farm. Digger sat down on a wing chair near the sofa. All the upholstery matched—there was a hand behind this house, and the hand behind his own was gone.

Some cider was passed around, a slight bit hard. A can of snuff. While they waited, the talk ran to dairy prices—still dropping no matter Hoover's promises. Or Governor Roosevelt's either.

"Still twelve thousand extra cans of milk a day!"

"Last milk check comin' in wasn't more'n a few dollars over the grain bill."

"If that."

"Or under."

Don and Jake arrived with David Freidman, a young lawyer from New York City. He was in his late twenties and wore a sheepskin-lined coat and a new brown-plaid cap. He shook hands around the room and then took the seat Jack offered.

Ed Whittaker read the minutes from the previous meeting: whether or not they were going to grade milk, the welcome tax on oleo, and the heavier than average precipitation rates. North Kortright put in poles for electric. When Ed finished the old business, there was some clearing of throats. The women came from the kitchen and stood in the doorway. Leenie was holding Rebecca face out, her gurgling the only noise in the room.

"Well, we knew it anyway," Wayne finally said. "Those of us was lookin'."

"But seein' it in the paper there," Jack added.

Henry spoke. "I called Schiowitz down in Wilkes-Barre. Pennsylvania just doesn't have the means to fight it anymore. They—and New Jersey too—were our strongest allies."

"They say the City will only use *flood* waters. What does Burch think a river is if it ain't water comin' off the mountain?"

"Rivers don't follow a norm."

"It's *all* flood water. But they ain't using the river *itself,* technically speaking."

They chuckled, nodded, and grunted, but found little comfort.

"Mr. Freidman here wants to help," Don said.

Freidman turned his cap in his hand. "The City will pay as little to each of you as it can get away with. I'm here to help you get your money's worth."

"Uriah has already called him," Don said.

Freidman continued, "It's the lower-river farms, your farms, in the closest proximity to the actual dam that will be condemned first."

Digger looked him over. "How long did you work for the City?"

"Two years."

The next morning after Digger finished milking, he found Freidman at the house, talking with Leenie. She was saying, "On the radio? Millay?"

"Yes. Reading her own. On Friday evenings."

"Poems right on the radio?" Her face was lit up, and Digger saw how Freidman was looking at her. His hair was all slicked back.

Freidman put out his hand, "Mr. Benton." But Digger walked by it and stood next to Leenie at the table.

"I'm not interested, Mr. Freidman, in any help you may be able to provide."

"But there are considerations, many considerations that could bring you the money you deserve. I've been talking to your niece here."

"I see that."

"She said this was your grandfather's farm."

"That's true."

"It must mean a lot to you, and we can use that to fight for what's rightfully yours. You have an old cemetery on this land?"

"No."

"It doesn't have to be formal. Any graves at all would do."

"I said no. And right now I suggest, Mr. Freidman, that you turn around and leave."

"Mr. Benton, you don't understand, I—"

Digger walked to the door and opened it, held out his arm, and waited till the young lawyer walked out.

"Well, ain't you the big man!" Leenie said. "He comes here tryin' to help and you run him off. Why? Because he's from the City? Because he's educated?"

"He's too young to help us."

"Young? Like me? I'm too young? And nothin's wrong with you bein' old?"

"You wanna run off with him?"

"What?"

"I seen him look at you."

"My God, Digger, are you jealous?" She covered her mouth. "You're jealous!" She laughed. "You're jealous."

"Alright, I'm jealous."

"That must mean you really do like me."

"You don't have to be educated to figure *that*, do ya?"

"But if you think I'd traipse off with that man, you don't know the first thing about me."

"Well, you were talkin' about poems and—"

"You look cute when you're jealous."

"Don't mock me."

"I'm not. I think you're handsome, even if you are too old." She brought her face up to his for a kiss.

12

Leenie was not a farm girl. She was not a mother. She was not a wife. She was not a river person or a town girl, and she no longer fit up on the hill. She was finished high school and was not yet close to college. And if she didn't watch out, this limbo could last forever. In love. Wrong love. Plain wrong and yet, *there.*

Since that meeting about the dam, Digger had grown more despondent. Each night after supper, he went to bed with Rebecca and lay there, waiting for her or not, she couldn't tell, but some nights she curled close behind him and held him till his breathing quickened. The edges of things receded, the world was fluid again, and what she could feel was what was.

One morning he was shaving at the kitchen sink in front of the small mirror hanging from a nail off the window frame. "It's your birthday Monday," he said. "You wanna go to the Grange dance Saturday night?"

"Dance with you? In front of people? You crazy?"

"I don't dance."

"And I suppose you gonna just set there watchin' me dance with some other men, havin' a grand ole time? That's the dumbest idea ever come from your mouth."

Digger rinsed his shaving brush and picked up his razor.

Leenie said, "I thought everyone in town knew how to dance."

On the morning of her birthday, a truck delivered a carton four feet high and wide. Digger helped the deliveryman carry it into the kitchen. After the man left, Leenie ran her fingers over the box. There, in bold letters, were her name and the farm address.

"Ain't you gonna open it?"

She took the butcher knife and slit the tape on the box. Inside was a phonograph, a real phonograph.

"Secondhand," Digger explained. "Charlie Weaver, he lost his job and had to sell it. It'd been a tenth-anniversary present for his wife, but since they were selling it, they threw in all the records—Jed Tompkins, Honey Duke, Jane Gray, Sam Jones."

"Where are we gonna put it?" Leenie asked.

"In the parlor."

They set it down in the far corner between two straight chairs pushed against the wall. Digger opened the console and fiddled with the needle. Leenie moved the coffee table back against the sofa. A few logs were left in the fireplace from when they closed up the parlor for the winter. Addie's picture was on the mantle, and Leenie picked it up. Addie was smiling slightly, holding on to her hat. A few brown curls fell along her cheek. She stared directly at the camera, and directly at Leenie too.

"We have two extra needles," Digger said, winding the motor.

Leenie set the picture back.

"How about Sam Jones?" he said, taking the record from its cover.

As the man's low, deep voice filled the room, Digger took her hand. "Maybe I'm not too old to learn."

Leenie looked up at him. "Or we can just pretend."

Digger started to sway and she rested her head against his shirt covered with hair from the horses and cows shedding, a thermometer in his front pocket. She closed her eyes. Sixteen years old with a baby about to cry, and here they were in a daylight hour, dancing.

As the grass grew bright and deep, and the trees leafed out, Leenie quietly positioned herself around a truth she didn't want to face. As she hoed and raked and weeded and carried water, it came to her what she had to do. And what she would not do.

She would not tell Digger, though he probably already suspected. He was staring at her lately, during mealtimes and in the evenings from his chair. But if she told him, he might bring up marrying again and she couldn't bear it. And she wouldn't go off and give the baby away either. She could take only one path, and though it would cause a crack in Digger's heart, he wouldn't break, she knew that.

Leenie had set herself a date, July first. Before daybreak Digger left for the barn, and she dressed, putting pants over her leggings, her dress over her pants, a blouse and sweater over her dress, and her coat over all that. In a small vanity case, she packed extra underwear, a pair of socks, a nightgown, a skirt, and her toothbrush. She passed her fingertips over the spines of the books on the dresser and chose Emily Dickinson's *Poems*. Then she took Rebecca, sleeping in a basket, and quietly set the basket inside the barn within earshot of the men.

She left the lantern burning on the kitchen table. Under it, she left a note: *Digger, I will be back. I had to do this. Love, L . PS: Don't worry about me—I'll be alright.*

Peg had on a new blue dress with a pretty red-and-gold-flowered print on the vestee, the pockets, and collar. She had new shoes that Norbert had picked out from his shoe store. "He wouldn't let me even *look* at old-lady ankle shoes."

She was perched on a stool by the tub, pouring cupfuls of hot water onto Leenie's back. Leenie had never sat in a fixed tub with faucets hot and cold. She couldn't stop crying. Let down, Peg called it. "You've been holdin' it all in, dear, and it's gotta come out one way or another. But I do think you should talk to Will. He could drive up, get Hettie. She could help you."

Leenie shook her head. "No. She knows my ma."

"Don't matter, Hettie keeps everyone's secrets." Peg turned on the water and held her hand under the spout and then turned it off. "We've run out of the hot."

Leenie lay back and the water rose around her shoulders. "Can't you do it?"

Peg shook her head. "But I can take you to a woman who helped me."

"Isn't there anything I can just swallow?"

"There's pennyroyal works maybe a quarter of the time. And once I was given slippery elm bark. They put a sliver of it up into me—it didn't work. And there's a whole list of other things people try, but this woman, she'll help you."

That evening Norbert came home carrying orange lilies he bought at the florist shop.

"For my niece." He held the flowers out to Leenie, who wondered at them because lilies hadn't even budded yet.

"Flowers travel," Peg said, "just like fruit, they travel north." She ran water into a vase. "Well, ain't this gonna be a big night for you. Ever eaten in a restaurant?"

Cobbler's was only a few minutes' walk, on Main Street, three streets over. Peg ordered her usual, a sirloin steak "as rare as they dare." Leenie read the menu over and over, and decided on the meat loaf and gravy with an extra scoop of mashed potatoes.

What shocked her the most was how bright the place was. The light didn't fall in circles but over everything evenly, across the backs of chairs and on the white tablecloths. The only hole of darkness she found was in the bathroom, before she turned on the switch. It was a miracle, electricity, and it made her feel buoyant, lifted up. She was no longer living in the dark ages as Frances would say—even her problem was going to be taken care of. Oh, wouldn't her sister who loved anything modern be hooting now. And yet the man waiting on them—a man in a suit who obviously knew her uncle well, called him not Sir or Mr. Henderson but Norb—he lit the candle in the center of the table, and Leenie thought that sweet, a candle lit not for the light at all but for the flame, as if in memory of the fire where light first came from.

"Have you been thinking of any college in particular, Leenie?" Uncle Norbert asked.

"No," she said shyly. "I don't know of any . . . yet."

It was hard to believe this was *her* uncle, that he was even related to her father. She'd seen him only once a year when he came to her home and hung his kill on the deer tree in the yard. Her daddy made fun of him behind his back, calling him the best-dressed hunter in the county—except for his old boots, he bought an entire outfit from Sears Roebuck every few years—but even her daddy couldn't deny that his brother was a good shot.

"There's a very fine school in Poughkeepsie," he said. "Vassar."

Leenie asked him about it.

"It's a woman's college. For smart women."

As her uncle continued, Leenie imagined buildings with

large doors surrounded by lawns and a few old oaks, students reading in the shade. It made her want to cry.

The waiter brought their suppers, and Leenie watched how Norbert ate, how he took a sip of water, how he set his fork down or brought it up to his mouth. She did whatever he did, all at the same pace, and she liked how long it made the food last.

"Did you know Sims was born in a brothel?" Peg said out of the blue. "But then he was given to a couple who'd taken Jesus into their hearts. It was Jesus told 'em to take the boy."

"Was it now?" Norbert winked at Leenie. Maybe her daddy's irreverence was a family trait.

"Yes, Jesus alone saved him." Peg rolled her eyes.

Norbert set his napkin beside his plate, he was finished. "Couldn't taking a youngster in come from an inherent sense of moral obligation? Or even a mother's good training?"

Leenie piped up. "Anything special you gotta hand right over to Jesus, otherwise people don't see it as worthy—maybe won't see it all."

Norbert smiled. "You're your father's daughter alright."

No, Leenie thought, it was Digger who had made her think like that.

"Your father was once a very smart man," Norbert added. "Before his habit took hold."

Daddy One, Daddy Two was what she and her sisters called their pa. Or sometimes just Either-Or, not knowing which father they were going to get. Leenie longed for the daddy who sometimes called her "the original one," sometimes "his quirky girl," sometimes just "the ponderer." "Now go ponder that," he'd say and she'd run off and sit with her feet in the stream, her eyes narrowed and her fist under her chin until she thought of something good enough to bring back to him.

That was all before his *habit* took hold—the word itself made the drunks seem smaller.

"I just couldn't tell him," Leenie said. She and Peg were in twin beds in the guest room.

"Will's a good man," Peg said.

"That's what I'm scared of."

Leenie's ma always talked about men like they were all the same. "You know men, they don't like touchin' water." Or, "Don't you mention there's garlic in that, not to the men." And though Leenie always dismissed what her ma said, now she too was thinking *men.* There she was with life in her womb and she was about to kill it. Men could strut around in the bright light and go off to war and kill people, then come home and get decorated. Women could make life but couldn't even mention the word *kill.* She wanted to talk to Digger, to set her mind and heart straight. But she couldn't. She was going into her own woods, carrying her own knife.

The next morning Peg set down a bowl of oatmeal in front of Leenie and said, "It's gonna cost, but Norb, he's willin' to pay."

"What! You told Uncle Norbert?"

"I had to, Leenie. Twenty dollars. Where you gonna find that kind of money if you don't wanna tell Will? And Norbert, he knows what it's like bein' underground."

Peg and Leenie walked to the edge of town and down a narrow dirt alley between some brick buildings. A woman wearing a navy-blue housecoat leaned from a doorway and waved them over. They followed her up a stairway and into a small kitchen. Off the kitchen was a room the size of a bed, but it didn't have a bed in it, it had a table raised up with cement blocks under the legs.

The woman pulled the curtains shut and turned on the ceiling bulb. She told Leenie she was going to give her a cervical punch. She would bleed for a few days and then miscarry. Then the woman gave Leenie two sheets, one for the table and one for her.

Leenie closed the door to the tiny room and undressed. She took care arranging the sheet, making sure it hung evenly off each side of the table before she lifted herself up. *Mama*, she whispered, and she lay back and waited.

PART III

I'd grown up killing, it wasn't that. Being the oldest, I'd killed my first chicken when I wasn't yet ten. Blood's never bothered me—flows into the dirt, turns black, and is gone. Bones don't either—the ground swallows them too.

This was different—smaller. Smaller than a thumbnail, like some tree frog in a swamp you can hear once the ground thaws. The swamp, though, was me.

Some say I don't know religion. But I know not all those born get to live, not all those conceived get to birth. And as I walk by the child graves (starting with my brother Wade's) and read the stones too, of the mothers, dead from birthing, and dead from not, I see a battleground no one plays the trumpet for. Walk by and tell me that ain't religion.

13

Of course she was pregnant. He should've let himself know it sooner. He hadn't asked her what was wrong, because he didn't want to intrude. But he should've known and, what? Offered to marry her? The thought embarrassed him. No, he wasn't embarrassed, he was ashamed. But who could she turn to?

She was smart and would've thought of Peg. He'd call Norbert or just go there. But first there was Rebecca—she wouldn't eat. He had to find Hettie.

Digger had never been to Hettie's house. Up on a knoll, it was small and unpainted, set back behind a stone wall four feet high. He knocked and Hettie called, "Come in." She was at her table eating bread with butter and jam. In a glass of water beside her was a pink peony lit from the sun coming through the opened curtains. He hadn't seen Hettie like this, wearing an ironed blouse and taking care of no one but herself.

He laid his cap on the table and set Rebecca on his knee. "Leenie left."

Hettie poured him coffee.

"Well," he added, "she's gonna come back. I think she went to see Peg Bridges."

"Pregnant," Hettie said. "When did she go?"

"Day before yesterday. In the mornin.'"

She studied Digger. "There's a woman I'm sure Peg knows. She helps women, girls who get into trouble."

He nodded.

"Different method than I use—I use plain soap—but—"

"Please come with me, Hettie."

"I might not be needed."

"Please."

Leenie lay asleep in the twin bed closest to the wall. Peg wrung out a cold washcloth and placed it on Leenie's forehead. Hettie set her bag down and picked up Leenie's wrist. "How long she been bleedin'?"

"Since yesterday afternoon."

"How many hours after?"

"A few."

"Miscarried yet?"

Peg shook her head.

Leenie moved her arms and made a small whimpering sound. She was in a fever. Digger sat down on the other bed next to the towels, sheets, oilcloth, and bedpan. Peg put her hand on his shoulder. "She's been callin' for you, Will," she said, and she and Hettie went out and left him with her.

"I'm here," he whispered. She was so pale he thought of Addie.

"Yes you are," she said, weakly.

He took her hand.

"I'm sorry," she said.

"It's not your fault," Digger said. "I'm sorry too."

"Couldn't tell you."

He brought her hand to his lips. "Don't worry about me. You rest now." He brushed back her hair from her forehead.

* * *

When Norbert came home from work, Digger told him, "I owe you."

"No, no, Willis, you've always been kind to me, you and Addie."

"Very least I can pay you back the money."

Norbert shook his head. "Is she any better?"

"Not yet."

They took turns watching over her. Every few hours Hettie took a small bottle and counted out drops onto Leenie's tongue—black haw and shepherd's purse for the bleeding, and birthwort, goldenseal, and myrrh gum to fight infection.

In the late morning, she miscarried, but the bleeding didn't stop and her fever was rising. It'd shot up to 103 during the night, and was still 101. Her pulse was racing.

"We gotta get a doctor," Digger said.

Peg came in from the bathroom, drying her arms with a hand towel. "Hent makes the women confess before he'll treat 'em."

"If we take her back to Schiffman," Hettie said, "she'll be bouncin' all that way in the truck. And then you got Sims to deal with. Probably some jail time there too—unless *you* got some sway over the reverend, Willis."

"How will Sims know?" Digger asked.

Peg and Hettie just looked at him.

"I can do for her," Hettie said.

That night, her fever held steady. By the next night, it was spiking to 104. Digger went down to Norbert's cellar and found a bottle of whiskey. He went out to where his truck was parked and sat in the driver's seat with his cap over his eyes to shade out the streetlight.

When he went back in the house, Hettie met him in the hall. "You been drinkin'."

"I'm alright."

"Her fever's worse, and she's been callin' for her mother. Will you go and bring Edith back? Peg will leave before she comes."

Digger agreed but thought that the love Leenie was calling for wasn't the love that was going to come.

Edith was cutting chives in the little garden off the back stoop. When she saw Digger, she straightened. "What happened?" she asked.

"Leenie's got a fever. She's been calling for you."

"Infection?"

He nodded.

"I know how you been livin'," she said. "From an abortion, ain't it?" She turned toward the house and he followed her in. "And to think Addie ain't been dead a year."

Digger took her arm and turned her to face him. "She needs you," he said.

"She's not my daughter."

He dropped her arm loose. "You don't know." He was shaking.

"What?"

"I forced myself on her."

Frances had been sitting on the bottom stair and heard it all. She watched while Edith unlaced her boots and put on her town shoes.

Someone was calling her. Why was someone always calling her? "Wake up, Leenie, come on. We're gonna sit you up now." It was Hettie.

But it was her mama's face. Her worried face. "Swallow. Just one more time, swallow."

"I think she's gonna be alright," Hettie said.

Well, of course I will, Leenie thought, there's electricity here. It was everywhere, in the walls, and coming from the ceiling, floating toward her in radiant skeins of light.

The next morning Leenie woke to her mother's snoring. Hettie sat on the vanity stool between the beds, looking tired. "Where's Peg?" Leenie asked.

"She left," Hettie said, "out of respect for your mother."

They were quiet until Leenie asked, "You thought I was going to die?"

"We thought you might, but you're gonna be fine."

Edith poured pitcherfuls of warm water over Leenie's back and shoulders. There was no water in the tub, because Hettie said it was too early for a real bath. Leenie closed her eyes and made *mmmm* sounds. She felt tired, but dreamy, and like a child again.

"It was the only thing I could think of," her mama said, "to get you out and to college." She scrubbed Leenie's arms. "You were always the smart one."

She started on Leenie's feet and calves. "I couldn't watch you stay at the farm and just fester. But, by God, he's gonna send you off to college now. Using you as a wife like that. Poor girl, you wasn't even sixteen."

Leenie sat up, but didn't say anything. She'd wait; she was too tired. She lay back again and rested and let her mama wash her.

What'd you tell her?" Leenie asked. She and Digger were on their way home.

"That I forced you. It was the only thing I could think of to get her to come."

It was a week since her ma had bathed her, and Leenie still hadn't corrected her.

"What about my daddy?" she said. "On his first drunk he'll probably come with his gun."

"Your ma ain't gonna tell him. I made a deal she won't wanna disturb."

The deal turned out to be a trade. Digger gave Edith his half-Percheron, Dan, and took Lady in foal off her hands.

"You made a trade? With my mother?" She wouldn't meet his eye.

"Well, you *wanted* that foal, didn't you?"

"Oh, Digger." She let out a long breath.

"Well, you won't have to hear your ma complain anymore about bein' stuck with a pregnant mare."

"And I thought you were a smart man." She was holding back tears. "She thinks you raped me. She thinks I didn't enjoy it. If I enjoyed it, she'd disown me. But as long as I'm miserable, she can still love me. She can love me *more* if I'm hurting like her. And she was eager to make a deal with the man she thinks raped me. Now you tell me what to think about *that*."

"I did everythin' I could," Digger said. "She might not be your first choice, but she's still the only mother you have. I was just tryin' to bring you back together."

Leenie was quiet, then said, "Well, I don't want her thinkin' that."

Digger went down to the cellar to run wire through the pipe coming from the spring—something was clogging it. Upstairs Leenie was putting Rebecca down for her afternoon nap. When they heard the knocking, Leenie from above, Digger from below, they each knew it was her daddy. Digger came up from the cellar and opened the door.

"What're you doin' to my daughter?" Sam said.

"It ain't what you think, Sam. Come on in."

Sam stepped inside. "She's gonna come with *me*, that's what's she gonna do. I ain't gonna let you ruin her."

"I'm stayin' here, Daddy."

"What?" Sam looked at his daughter standing in the doorway to the parlor.

"This is my home now."

Sam looked back at Digger and then to Leenie again, and nodded slowly. "I see," he said.

Digger pulled out a chair. "Why don't you sit down."

They sat at the table and Leenie moved the vase of peonies so she could see her pa, Daddy One, sitting across from her. She saw him see Addie's clothes.

"You're wearing—"

"Yes," she said. "And everything, it was with my own free will."

Sam was silent, then finally said, "Why'd you say what you said, Willis?"

"Edith—"

"Yes, I know," Sam said, raising a hand. Then he cocked his ear, something he did when he was thinking or about to tell a story. "Why don't I take you home, Leenie, so you can talk to your ma. The baby can do without you for a night."

Leenie looked down at the table. They were both looking at her.

"I know she ain't easy," Sam said, "but your mother had a few dreams of her own when she was young." He sighed. "Till she met me."

Leenie looked up. "Alright. I'll go and get a few things."

When she came back to the kitchen, Sam was telling Digger the story about the stones. She'd heard his version before.

"When she was real little, she got it in her mind to give me a special stone before I'd go off loggin' every fall, so whenever I missed her, I could rub the stone. Now in the beginnin' she'd give me a stone that could fit in my pocket. But then she got older and decided a stone that fit in my pocket wasn't big enough. So she dragged a rock the size of a book to the back stoop for me to take on my trip. So I carried it off down the road wavin' bye and smilin', and at the foot of the hill I tucked the rock behind the last post of Charlie Owen's fence. When I came home in the spring, I could find it and carry it up to the house and show her how I was carryin' it around the whole time. Well, that worked till one winter there was a flood that drove an acre of river rock up against the fence. I knew Leenie would know exactly what her rock looked like, so I picked out one as best I could, and she knew. She was only seven or eight, and she said, It ain't the stone! You lost the Leenie stone! That was the last stone she ever give me."

As they drove out the driveway in Osmer's Model T, Sam eyed the flower bed. "You planted those marigolds?" he asked.

"Yes," Leenie said. "I found Addie's seeds in the shed. Her tomatoes too."

Sam shook his head and smiled, but didn't say any more. As they passed over the bridge, a few boys were at the swimming hole, climbing the rocks and flying off the rope.

"I started it, Daddy. I *wanted* it."

"Like me," he said, "you were heedin' the call."

Leenie finished the phrase in her head, one of her ma's: *the call of the ne'er-do-well.* "Daddy," she said, "did you get Ma pregnant? I mean before?"

He didn't answer and she knew. Finally, he said, "Don't tell your sisters."

"But *I* wasn't early."

"No you weren't."

"Did Hettie—"

"Yes," he said. "That was your ma's dark angel."

The two sisters sat on a knoll where the sun hit, watching the fog lift from their ma's orchard. "Luxuriant," Leenie had called the morning, not having to worry about a baby. She waited for Frances to roll her eyes, but she didn't.

"Frances?"

Her sister sat up, twirling a blade of timothy in her mouth.

"Was it Ma told Daddy? 'Bout my condition?"

Frances shook her head.

"Who was it then, told him?"

Frances held her elbows and rocked herself.

"Didn't you know I could be put in jail? For two years! And the woman too. And Peg! All of us!"

Frances's eyes teared up. "I was on our spot on the stairs when Uncle Willis came in. I thought, I thought . . . Pa could stop it."

"Pa's got a drunk tongue. Who knows who he told before he came to us. And now Digger's name—"

"Well, how was I supposed to know it wasn't true?"

Leenie nodded. "I know." Then she patted her sister's hand. "We've both heard a lot from that place, haven't we?"

Frances was silent for a while, then asked, "Does it hurt, lovin'?"

Leenie's face flushed. "A little at first. But there's a reward."

Frances waited while Leenie took her time.

"A little angel with a tiny torch reaches in through your breasts and then lights her way down into your stomach, making it tingle in a big circle around your belly button just like whiskey does, and then finally she goes all the way down, sets fire to your privates, and flies away. She's gotta make it out quick or she'll get burned."

Frances giggled. "Does she have a name, this angel?"

"Wouldn't know. She does everythin' without sayin' a word."

Leenie found her ma in the barn putting Dan away. So there'd be no little ears around, Frances took Mary and Janey up to the meadow to pick strawberries.

While her ma was brushing Dan's legs, Leenie said, "There's something I have to tell you."

"I know," Mama said, setting down the brush. "Your pa didn't want me to be surprised, he wanted me to think on it."

"Have you?"

"Yes." But then she picked up the harness and carried it to the back, the traces dragging along the cement. *Any of your children dragged good leather like that, you'd wring their necks,* Leenie thought, but then she softened. She put Dan back into his stall while her ma hung the bridle and reins on one hook, the belly band and breeching on the other. As her ma walked back toward her, Leenie said, "I hated you were thinkin' that about him."

"I've known Willis a long time. All through Addie . . . I thought her such a child then too."

Leenie met her eye. "Ma, Daddy told me. About you."

Mama nodded. "I never listened to my mother. Not till it was too late. But she always said, Honor the dead by livin'. You go out now, Leenie, and live, you hear? You make a life."

Leenie looked away. She had come here to forgive her ma, but there was nothing to forgive her for.

14

Digger and some other men were helping Wayne move his barn up to his grandfather's land on Bussy Hollow. "Now that the valley's good as gone," Wayne said. His nephew George was there to help and Ed Whittaker and Jack Bryant and old Uriah. Digger brought Burdett too, but with the agreement Wayne would pay him. Jimmy said he'd show up, but no one expected him—he was already building another still in the woods behind his brother's house. As the rest of the men worked their way down the long side, prying off the siding and throwing it on the ground, Digger stayed in the back, yanking nails from the boards and sorting them into piles—what was good to use just as it was, what was nothing but kindling, and the in-between pile, the largest.

Uriah had come only to stand and talk, his main job now, as befit his age. "These big-talkin' reverends, they come and go." After a pause, he added, "And Jimmy, he'll keep a more watchful eye now."

Digger wiped the sweat off his forehead. Sims had dropped by his farm a couple times lately, first to give Becca a baby blanket crocheted by a woman in his congregation, and then to invite Leenie to a church party. "There'll be a lot of young mothers there," Sims told her.

"Don't waste your time worryin' over Sims," Uriah said. "Focus on gettin' somethin' for your farm." Digger went on sorting and Uriah continued, "Wayne says Freidman's gonna drop by later. You talk to him yet?"

Digger shook his head and threw a board onto the good pile.

"He's gettin' for Wayne as much for his farm *without* the barn as he would with it. Better talk to Freidman soon. By next spring, they'll start to condemn and your farm will be one of the first."

"Alright," Digger said. The dam was coming and all you could do was get your money and move.

Leenie was trying to braid her hair in front of the small shaving mirror by the sink. She didn't like it that she cared so much now what Digger thought. And the baby was about to wake up. If she could spend just one day alone, one day not being touched, or being touched just at night.

At noon, Digger came in and they sat down to enjoy the first tomato of the season together, but Leenie couldn't eat. "Digger, I—" She let out a long breath.

"What?"

"I . . . I'd like a . . ."

"What?"

"A dress," she said quickly.

He smiled. "A dress? That all?"

"I mean . . ." she stammered, "of, of my own."

"Walk right down to Alma's. Today, this afternoon. Take Becca and go. I'll go to the attic, get some bills for you."

"You don't think it's spoiled of me?"

"Spoiled? Heavens no. You been walkin' around in clothes too big for you, even I can see that."

She lowered her head, but the smile she was trying to hide broke across her cheeks.

After Leenie left with the baby carriage for town, Digger went up into his old bedroom. He wanted to surprise Leenie. It was only right she should use Addie's vanity table, have a good-sized mirror. But before he could move the table an inch, he sat down on the bed, *their* bed he hadn't slept in for months, almost a year. Maybe it was the dirty windows facing the road or the dust covering the bedside tables and the headboard, covering what had been the bright shining room of his life. How he wanted to talk to Addie now, wanted, strangely, to tell her about Leenie. All winter, he'd felt like a boy around her, ready anytime to roll in the hay. What would Addie think? She was his sturdy, sensible girl. Always loved to deliver advice, didn't she—he should talk more at the Bureau meetings, he should preach less, especially to her. He certainly wasn't preaching now. Would his wife even recognize him? Would she love him? But Addie was dead, and he was alive. He didn't want to turn back now, he couldn't.

When Leenie first heard the thunder, she picked up the pace, rolling the carriage right on past Sal's toward Alma's on the upper end of town. She'd had her eye on the red dress she'd seen in the store window.

Alma opened the door as Leenie backed the wheels up the final step. Becca was starting to wake and Leenie rolled the carriage in front of the counter and rocked it.

"First, dear, I see you need a dress that fits," Alma said. "Why the both of you could live in that blouse." Alma was a tall, thin woman who'd never been married but, everyone always added, had very fine taste and a dressmaking sister in the City who kept Alma up on the new fashions.

"I was thinkin' about the dress in the window," Leenie said.

"The ruby one?"

Leenie nodded and gradually slowed the carriage to a standstill.

"Let's just check your size." Alma slipped her measuring tape off the hook behind the counter and Leenie followed her into the fitting room—two screens set up in the corner. "My my, dear, you are blessed."

When Alma lifted the dress off the rack, Leenie ran her fingertips over it—just the feel of satin. It was the line, Alma was saying, the graceful line the yoke front gave it—and it would show off Leenie's full bosom.

Leenie put it on and stood in front of the mirror.

"Sharp," Alma said, "very sharp." She'd have to take it in along the side, Leenie having such slim hips, not like some women these days. But since it was raining out, it was likely no other customers would be coming by and Alma could do it right then in the back room. Leenie could feed Becca while she waited.

Alma cleared off a chair for them, lit a lantern, and sat down at her machine. While her hands moved, her lips did too. First about the Presbyterian choir, then about the Hoover days. As soon as the dam got built and Alma got her money, she was going to live with her sister down in the City.

"And it was nice to see your mother in here, was it the day before yesterday?"

"My mother?"

"Yes, to buy some fabric—for Frances, the one leaving?"

"Leavin'?"

"Going to live with some aunt of yours up near Catskill? Where she can finish high school?"

Leenie was stunned. How could *they* come all the way down here from Mary Smith and not even stop . . . Frances was leaving?

"Frances pleaded for the blue, the Canton blue, you can see

a piece of it there on the shelf." Alma took a pin from her lips. "Oh, how she begged, and your mother, she finally gave in."

It wasn't raining anymore but there was still a charge in the air. Main Street was shining black, and water rushed down the gutters on each side. She was relieved she hadn't worn the dress home, it would've been wet already. She turned onto Church Street. The wind was coming up, stirring the tops of the maples, and the clouds were getting dark. Then it started to pour. She snapped the corduroy shield over Becca and tucked the package with her new dress in between the cushion and the wicker. She half walked, half ran. Becca was screaming and she still had a mile and a half to go. A black truck pulled off the road, and the driver rolled the window partway down. "What's a purdy girl like you doing in this weather?"

"Tryin' to get home."

"Better git in 'fore you both catch the death of cold. I'll set the carriage in the back."

She grabbed Becca and her new dress from the carriage and climbed into the cab. The rain was deafening. Becca was soaked. The man got in and slammed the door. He was heavyset and had a very red face. "So where am I takin' you, Miss?"

"The first farm on the River Road, it's not much more'n a mile."

"The Benton farm?"

"Yes."

"So you're the girl," he said. "I heard about you." He slowed and turned into the backyard of Reverend Sims's church.

Leenie thought about running, but she and the baby were soaked, and the man stayed close, ushering her through the rain to the rectory. Mrs. Sims opened the door. She was plump, in a yellow apron with small blue flowers. She smiled and took

Leenie's hand. "Ooh so cold, dear, and you're shiverin', let's get you warmed up." At the kitchen doorway Leenie looked behind her, and the man had disappeared.

Mrs. Sims poured her a cup of tea. "Now, sit right down, dear. You want milk with it, don't you?"

Leenie nodded, laying her package on the table. The brown paper had gotten wet and she hoped the dress wouldn't have any water stains.

Mrs. Sims poked at the fire, then bustled about, getting a plate of butter cookies for Leenie.

"Thanks," Leenie said.

"And now for the baby," Mrs. Sims said. "Let's see what we can do." She went out and came back, carrying a box labeled 1–2 YRS. "I'm afraid this is as little as we go, there've been so many newborns lately." She untied the string and rummaged through it till she found some diapers. Then she lifted out a white smock with yellow embroidery on the collar.

"That's lovely," Leenie said, taking another cookie.

"A tad too big, but she'll grow into it, won't she? The little darlin'." Mrs. Sims laughed as she lifted Becca from Leenie's lap. "Now, you just rest, dear."

Mrs. Sims changed Becca, rolled her wet clothes into a ball and tied it with twine. Then she pulled out a chair next to Leenie and sat with the baby, seesawing her arms and cooing, blowing on her ears and cheeks, making Becca laugh.

A few minutes later Reverend Sims came in, and his wife stood up with Becca in her arms. "We'll just leave you and the reverend for a little while so you can talk."

Leenie raised her hand, but Mrs. Sims hurried out.

Digger had decided he and Burdett would repair the broken boards in the bull pen. It could still be five or six years before they started building the dam, and then another few before it was finished. What was he going to do, let everything just break around him?

They worked into the afternoon, listening to the rain pummel the tin roof. Finally, Digger stopped and looked out at the rain falling in a sheet from the overhang. Burdett said, "I'll bring the cows down, Mr. Benton, if you wanna go pick Miss Leenie up."

Digger figured she'd be at Sal Placieri's, eating a plate of spaghetti, or at Alma's. But she wasn't at either place.

He drove up Main Street and onto Church. He drove down to the River Road and back to the farm, and then not knowing what else to do, he drove into town again. On his third trip he noticed a black truck with the wicker carriage in the back, parked at Sims's church.

"You're still Miss Henderson?" Sims said. "You're not Mrs. Benton yet, are you?"

She wrapped her palms around the teacup.

Sims held a Bible in the crook of his arm. "For Adam was first formed, then Eve," he quoted. "And Adam was not deceived. But the woman being deceived was in the transgression." He paused. "And you, Miss Henderson, are also in transgression."

She wasn't going to lift her eyes.

"Did you hear me?"

She nodded.

"Can you tell me what I said, Miss Henderson?"

"That Eve was in the wrong."

"And what else?"

"That it's a wrong runnin' so deep in creation, it's run right through to me."

"I don't like your tone, Miss Henderson."

"I don't particularly like yours either, Reverend."

She tightened her grip on the cup to stop her hands from shaking. She had to get hold of herself.

Sims went on. "Is there any hope, any salvation for a girl who can shamelessly seduce a grieving man?" He lifted a hand in the air. "And to our great dismay, we have been told that after having been impregnated by Mr. Benton you destroyed your own flesh and blood." He held the Bible to his chest. "But the merciful love of the Lord Jesus Christ is unbounded, and with repentance, genuine and absolute submission . . . What we need to know is who helped you perform such a heinous crime?"

She grabbed her dress and stood to move toward the door.

"Now you just sit down and hear me out, Miss Henderson. I'm here to help you." His tone softened. "All you've done can be forgiven."

There was no fighting him. He pushed her gently back into the chair.

"Leenie, it's not you who's bad. Jesus knows that and *I* know that." His voice lifted. "Heal Thy daughter, O Lord—"

The door opened and Digger walked in.

"Well, well," Sims said, patting his chest, "this is no surprise."

Digger looked around. "Where's Rebecca?" Leenie pointed and Digger said, "Go get her. We're goin' home." Leenie nodded and hurried out, but stayed behind the door listening.

Digger turned on Sims. "What are you doin'? Stalkin' her with your religion?"

"Oh, Will, don't *you* go getting high-minded on me. If I were you, I'd get down on my knees and repent. We can throw the full weight of the law against you. For statutory rape."

"Why don't you just stay away from her," Digger said.

"I think *you* should make sure she's gone from your farm by fall."

"That's for her to decide."

"Her? Tell me, Will, were you thinkin' about *her* when you impregnated her? I'm sure you were thinking hard. Why *she* doesn't belong on your farm and you know that."

"You think you know all about our lives."

"Evil has a way of seeping into every crack it can find. But you should know your girl walked in here of her own accord."

"And who owns the black Ford parked out back?"

"A kind man trying to help. Like Hettie Brower was trying to help. Did you ask Hettie to kill that fetus?"

"She had nothin' to do with it."

"Then I know who did."

Digger opened the family Bible to Records, to the last entry, in Addie's handwriting.

Adelaide Hansen married to Willis Benton, August 7, 1926

He touched her name, then got a pen from his desk and wrote what he couldn't before:

Adelaide Hansen Benton, died November 1, 1930
Rebecca Hansen Benton, born November 1, 1930

He shut the Book. The heft of it recalled the wonder he felt as a boy when he read about David and Goliath, Abraham and Isaac, Jacob and Esau. Always, eventually, even the proudest man prostrated himself. It's that false clinging to virtue, Digger thought, makes us treacherous. His boy-mind had been soft as loam, and the words pounded their way into him. Oh, he'd been blinded by his love for God, *his* God as Leenie once said, and he had recoiled from the pronoun. The God of Abraham. After Addie died, Digger had leaned right against

Him and He didn't budge. But now Digger felt both he and his God were being washed away.

Leenie stood in the doorway. She held out her arms and let them fall to her sides. "I'm trying to slough off Sims," she said. "We can't let him march into our lives, ruin our home."

The words *our home* took him by surprise. "I need to talk to you," he said.

"Well, I'm not stoppin' you. Not yet anyway." She dropped into the kitchen chair beside him.

"I do love God. I love Him, though I know He's greedy. Headstrong. Jealous—"

"This is Sims we're talkin' about, not God."

"All I know is it ain't a perfect Book and He ain't a perfect God, but He's all I got."

She reached her hand toward him. "I love how you love Him. Though He does strong-arm you about."

He took her hand. "Why, look at that dress. You come down to show it to me? Let's see."

She stood and twirled for him, but then she stopped. "It's been a long time since you've, since we've—"

"I didn't wanna hurt you."

"I think I'm all healed. We could at least try. Before Becca wakes." And she smiled her night smile he hadn't seen for a long time.

Afterward, she couldn't sleep. She'd forgotten how much she missed him—him in that way. When you're loving, she smiled to herself, you're in a different world with different laws. And the two of them, they fall in together. It's his *mass,* she thought, it pulls her right to him.

But now Digger lay on his back snoring, and Sims's words were going through her head, "Why, *she* doesn't belong on your farm and you know that." Those words had broken Digger. From then on, Sims had him.

She slipped out of bed, dressed in the dark, and headed for the river. In the light of the half-moon she walked past the Joe-Pye and sat on her rock. The water was moving faster than usual from the digging downstream. They didn't just scoop out the gravel from the last flood, Digger had said, they were cutting the channel deeper and straighter, and it sucked the water down from upstream and washed the bank away.

She drew her knees up and held them. She wanted to stay here forever, watching how the bank changed, or didn't, until it disappeared entirely under the waterline. And then what? Then Digger would find another farm. And she would be a farmer's wife, tending her tomatoes and sewing on buttons and waiting for milk to sour so she could bake another chocolate cake. Could she do it? Did she want to do it? She wanted to want to. Since she first learned the word *college,* that there was such a lucky place in this world, she had wanted to be there more than anything else, but she'd never imagined *this,* this that she would have to give up. She squeezed her knees hard, as if she could hold in her heart, but she couldn't.

She knew too well what her grandma meant, *honor the dead by livin'.* Like Digger's grandpa too—he'd bury his dead animals where he wanted his best crop, and not for the calcium in the bones either, but because, he told his grandson, death itself is a fertilizer. She hadn't understood that at all, not till now, now that she was carrying her own dead. Small though it was, it gave her something to live for. *You go out now, Leenie, and live, you hear?* Though she felt cut in two by a hay knife, she couldn't not hear.

It was almost dawn when she got back to the house. Digger was sitting by the stove, poking at the coals.

"Would me tellin' you I loved you help?" he said.

"Maybe."

"Well, I do."

She stood near him warming her hands.

"You love me? Your old crazy uncle?"

She leaned close to him, and touched his face. "Yes, I do."

"Don't you wish that were all it took?" he said.

"But it *is* somethin', Digger."

"Yes, it is. It is somethin'."

When Leenie got back from the station, Digger was in the yard by the milk house, one leg on each side of Becca crawling toward the stone step.

"Frances's train come in on time?" he asked, not looking up.

"Digger," Leenie said. "I have to leave. Now."

He snatched Becca up and turned around. "What? Now?"

"Well, soon. I can't even walk into town without wonderin', Do they know me? They against me? The lady selling Frances her ticket. Even in Uriah's store." She didn't mention the last thing her sister had said before disappearing into the train, "I'd rather die than end up like Ma."

"It'll settle down soon enough. People start to forget."

She shook her head. "It's time." And he saw by her face that she was already gone.

They went indoors and she heated up some of last night's supper. They ate in silence. *How would she go,* she wondered, *how would she eat.* Finally Digger leaned back from the table and said, "We'll call Norb. He knows people who can help." Then he patted her on the shoulder and left for the barn. She picked up the carrots Becca had thrown on the floor, set the dishes in the sink. Digger was driving the tractor out the gate on his way to harvest the buckwheat, his face lit up under his hat by the low-angle light. *How would she sleep? Sleep alone?*

* * *

The word *soon* hung in the air, but no day or time was mentioned. Not until Jimmy came to the house and told Digger that Peg's ma, Harriet, had died and was to be buried in Liberty. "On account of all the graves here gonna be moved." Jimmy waved his hand. "It's all goin', Will, all changin'."

"We'll be there," Digger said, thinking how easy it was to say *we* and knowing that meant Leenie would start to pack.

"You should take some of Addie's books," he said, "and leave what you want for Mary."

"How we gonna do it?" she asked.

"You can't write me," he said.

"What?"

"If you write me, then I'll know as soon as you stop that you've stopped . . ." They could hear the door on the woodshed slapping against its frame.

"I can't promise that," she said and went into the parlor. He heard the books dropping onto the floor—two piles, one for her, one for her sister.

He leaned back on the chair and closed his eyes. Maybe the wind would die down and not ruin his corn.

I did go to New York City and then to Vassar and after a few years, I could pass as educated. But in truth, the knowledge I picked up never sunk in—it sat on top the way cream does. What college didn't change was how I looked at the world, which was from the ground up. The ground—and not an idea of the ground, but as Digger liked to say, the very ground—was there beneath me, and that seemed to be enough, I didn't want God to come to my aid.

Still, I was a proud gal when in June of 1936, in front of my Uncle Norb and a rich friend of his, Mrs. J. P. Wagoner, who each paid a third of my way (Digger paid the other third), and my sister Mary, I graduated with a Bachelor of Arts degree. And within a week, I took a job as a stenographer in the Poughkeepsie town court.

I didn't write Digger once. I had made him that promise. Norb gathered the funds and sent the checks and kept me posted about all the doings on the farm. Lady had a filly shortly after I left and Digger named her Cash. She was breeched and he pulled her out by her back legs, and then when she was not even a year old, he heard Lady calling and ran into the barn and found little Cash outside the stall, the door still latched and not a board loose. She grew into a long-legged, wide-chested beauty like her sire, and Digger was offered for her from a man in Port Jervis $100 (one-sixth the cost of one semester), but he refused to sell her.

Digger kept visiting Peg in Liberty and eventually they married. Norb and Jimmy were their witnesses, one toasting with brandy, one with moonshine.

Through David Freidman, I kept up with the prolonged and elaborate correspondence between the river farms and the New York City Board of Water Supply. Six and a half years after I left, it was announced that the 489 acres of the Benton Farm were finally being condemned and would bring Digger $19,500, versus the measly $13,000 the City first offered. Freidman wrote me the exact date the title was to be turned over, and on April 14, 1938, I took the three trains back to Pepacton and then walked the last bit to the farm.

But the farm wasn't a farm anymore. Teddy had died a few years back, the cows were sold off before winter set in, though you could still see manure where the snow had melted. Johnny, Lady, and Cash too had been sold at auction and there was no hog, no chickens, nothing left but a few barn cats too wild to hold. The tractor was gone, along with the wagon, the corn planter, the sickle bar, and the harrows. There were still a few parts left in the shed, half a doodlebug Digger had started building but didn't finish, hay in the hayloft, some buckets here and there, and a stool in the milk room. "Just gonna get burned," Digger said. He was just as wiry, but more gray, more wrinkled, crow's-feet about his eyes and a smile held even closer to himself. Peg was as beautiful as ever, with salt-and-pepper hair and wearing an apron sprinkled with perfume. She hugged me and made me twirl around so she could see every inch of me, then hugged me again.

Before Becca got home from school, the three of us walked up to Addie's grave, to her stone that was going to be covered with water. Digger hadn't ever wanted anyone else to see it, thinking it was secret and solid and permanent, like he had imagined God was. The river too he imagined was something else, something with its own power and will and life, certainly not something that could be stoppered up.

I recognized Becca's face right away but of course she didn't recognize me. Seven years old and quite a character. "Why is it always Sunday getting the attention?" she said. "Why not Tuesday? Doesn't it work just as hard?" Red was her favorite color, though she put her hand on her hip and added, "I'm not ruling out yellow."

We ate a supper of cold ham and potato salad Peg had kept down in the cellar by the spring. We set our plates on our laps in what was almost a bare kitchen, with only a few of Digger's mother's chairs they hadn't sold or moved. Digger kept looking at me and shaking his head, but some days are like funerals, you either show up or you don't, and you have to show up on the very day to have it matter.

Digger swore he wasn't ever going to farm again, and they moved north to Greene County where for a few years he drove a truck, but then some land just south of Schoharie got his attention.

Three months later they bought 374 acres of bottomland, where he and Peg lived out the rest of their lives.

I lived in three different cities, Boston, Minneapolis, and finally Chicago, teaching both high school English and college literature. I did my best to fall in love with another man, and thought I did, twice, once with a man who turned out not as smart as he seemed despite all the facts he had at his disposal, and then with another who actually was smart in every way that counts, but turned out mean. I traveled through much of Europe and even visited Tokyo and Kyoto on an exchange program. But almost every summer I came back to the Schoharie Valley and stayed at Digger and Peg's farm, a place neighbors and friends walked in and out of freely.

When Peg became too lame in her hips to do even simple cooking, I decided to retire and take care of them. Peg was eighty-six years old when she had an aneurysm in her sleep and died. She had said death would be an adventure and you could tell by the wonder in her face that she saw it that way right to the end. She lost all her wrinkles in death and she would've been grateful for that. A year later, on the first of June in 1982, five days shy of his ninety-third birthday, Digger fell cutting brush and broke his back. For three months, I stayed by his bedside reciting him psalms and poems. His hands still had a powerful grip and if I steadied him he could lift himself in and out of the tub. Shortly before he went unconscious, he said, "It's time, Leenie, for you to go out and explore the world. I'll stay right here," and then he almost laughed. When he died,

I laid along the length of his body until all its heat was gone. This time, I was the one who was left.

Becca begged me not to call the undertaker until she arrived, which she managed to do all the way from St. Louis eight hours later. What she had wanted most was to hold his hands again. They had so much capacity, she said.

Peg wanted her ashes spread around her roses, Digger wanted his thrown into the Pepacton. It took a few years but Becca and I finally brought him back during the summer of '88. There'd been a drought and you could see remnants from the bridges in both Union Grove and Arena where the reservoir was shallower, even the stumps from the trees that had lined their Main Streets. Down through Shavertown and halfway to Pepacton, foundations were showing, a loading dock, a few hay ramps—I couldn't tell whose was whose, but I did spot the top of what they said was an Indian burial mound behind Ed Whittaker's, though no one found any more arrowheads there than they did on any other farm.

You couldn't see Digger's place, of course, it was too close to the dam, you could only just sense Addie's ridge right beneath the water. It was illegal for us even to be standing on the bank but I threw his ashes in anyway. What could they do to us now? I was already seventy-three years old and they say nothing on Earth's cleaner than ashes.

AUTHOR'S NOTE

This novel is based on the flooding of four towns in the western Catskills of New York—Pepacton, Shavertown, Arena, and Union Grove—to supply water to New York City. The local newspapers were abuzz with the planning and approval of the Pepacton Reservoir in 1931; I shortened the timeline of its protracted execution. Though many of the characters' names might appear familiar, none are based on real people. I use place-names I know and am fond of, but they are mixed and matched in a way that is adamantly inaccurate.

ACKNOWLEDGMENTS

With deep gratitude to:

James Hillman, for the power and poetry of his ideas;
Margot McLean, for her love of what matters;
Judith Katz, for her exquisite ear;
Ani Helmick, for her careful, extensive attention;
Annette Schultz, for the story's inception;
Mimi McGurl, for being there;
Lisa Marfleet, for her close, deep readings;
Jean Naggar, for her persistence;
Alice and Robert Jacobson, for their historical compilations of the river valley beneath the Pepacton;
Tom Jenks, for his incomparable literary sensibility and merciless editing;
and Eric Hamerstrom, for his manifest love.

ABOUT THE AUTHOR

Mermer Blakeslee is an author, teacher, skier, and gardener. She has been awarded three New York Foundation for the Arts Fiction Fellowships, and her second novel, *In Dark Water*, was selected by Barnes & Noble for its Discover Great New Writers series. "Leenie," an excerpt from *When You Live by a River*, won the Narrative Prize. Blakeslee's nonfiction book, *A Conversation with Fear*, is based on her work with fearful skiers. A former member of the National Alpine Team for the Professional Ski Instructors of America, Blakeslee was born, raised, and still lives in the Catskill Mountains.

OPEN ROAD
INTEGRATED MEDIA